GULAG

BOOK 4: WARLORD

XAVIER THERG

GULAG

BOOK 4: WARLORD

XAVIER THERG

Published by AOIX Press,
An imprint of White Media Works
San Diego, California

ISBN 978-1-64145-128-4

Other Works by Xavier Therg

The Bio-Mech War
An existential war between biologicals and mechs.

1: Orphan Rangers	10: Orange Crush
2: Clone Pods	11: Iron Termites
3: Space Turtles	12: Black Claw
4: Teardrop Bottles	13: Hard Landing
5: Blue Iguanas	14: Smiley War
6: Crabb World	15: Nowhere Man
7: Big Teeth	16: Dawn Fire
8: Lightning Moths	17: Laughing Boar
9: Galactic Xoo	18: Lost Cohort

The Transub
The resurrection of humankind
inside quantum portals.

1: Proxima	6: Spegellandet
2: Q-Port System	7: Recall Plateau
3: Algae War	8: Lost and Found
4: Q-Port Spider	9: Breakup Islands
5: Awams Refugee	10: Q-Port Makers

Gulag
Two million cons set free to
live or die by their own rules.

1: Survivor	11: *Mechas* *
2: Oil King	12: *Defenders* *
3: Mutants	13: *Hybrids* *
4: Warlord	14: *Spacehab* *
5: A.I.	15: *Rangers* *
6: *Whipped* *	16: *Stims* *
7: *Warder* *	17: *Chimeras* *
8: *Warmonger* *	18: *Constitution* *
9: *Armada* *	19: *Chosen* *
10: *Breakout* *	20: *Unbound* *

* coming soon.

Table of Contents

Episode 1 – Red

Eduardo Dios stood at the top of the airplane slide. In high-tech suits, some silver and some invisible, prisoners at the bottom chanted, "*Jump, jump, jump!*" Cons at the bottom scrambled off the slide while others behind Eduardo grumbled and pushed. Breathing deeply of the hot desert breeze, a friend from Avenal State Prison stood next to him.

"Free at last! Eh, Eduardo?" Pedro jumped on the slide, arms crossed over his chest.

Free at last. Eduardo stretched his neck to drink in the sky. Sharp white clouds cut at him like knives. A con behind him punched Eduardo in a kidney. He fell in a ball of flailing limbs. Around him were mocking laughs as cons pulled Eduardo to his feet to clear the bottom. Sacrificing rubber slides, engines were already revving to spirit the wide body jet away.

Wrapped head to toe in a green metal suit, a con pulled Eduardo free of the crowd. He yelled over the noise, "You're C block, right?" The con's face was hidden behind a face shield and Eduardo didn't recognize the voice.

When the question repeated, Eduardo nodded.

"C block is red. Paint your suit."

A few colored suits of red, green, blue and yellow were mixed in with the silvers. Like they had in the largest state prison in California, his gang was already organizing inside the gulag. When

Eduardo shrugged ignorance, the man yelled, "Open the front and I'll show you."

A tutorial Eduardo watched on the plane said that the shrouds would only open for the owner. A catalytic converter, or "cat", welded to the flap inside would produce food and water from any organic material stuffed into the hopper. Cons were relatively safe as long as they stayed sealed inside.

When Eduardo didn't move, the con laughed and unsealed the front of his own shroud. The young Black man swiveled a metal box that was attached to a flap. He tapped on the screen on one side. "You know how to turn on the cat, right?"

"Of course!"

"Here's the sequence."

As the man tapped through menus, his shroud changed colors from green to silver to white to invisible. Eduardo said, "I want that one."

The con turned green again. "La Fuerza needs to secure the area first. You're red."

Eduardo pulled his arms through the sleeves and looked down the billowing neck of the shroud to repeat the sequence in private. When his shroud was red, the man pounded him on the back. "There's another jet landing. Gather La Fuerza and have them code their suits to their facility."

As the man turned away, Eduardo yelled, "Wait! What's the code?"

"There's a message from El Jefe in your cat."

When Eduardo looked blank, the man sighed. "Here's the menu sequence for messages."

Avenal State Prison in Central California was divided into six independent facilities labeled A – F. La Fuerza was the only gang with a presence in all six, and El Jefe was on top. Eduardo hoped to take that position someday; at twenty-nine he was already captain of C block. Correction, those days were over. La Fuerza was history. They competed on a much bigger field now.

Until Eduardo figured out the rules, he might as well use the existing infrastructure. As Eduardo jogged to greet the next plane full of cons, he opened the message from El Jefe.

He tried to memorize the color scheme: blue, green, red, yellow, white, and black. Ugly, El Jefe had no imagination. Through the cat, any color, symbol, or picture could be reflected onto the outside of the suit. When Eduardo had his own gang, they would stand out like peacocks.

As the plane skidded to a stop, emergency doors popped open. The slides were inflated in bursts of pressurized air. Cons queued at the top of the ramp. In Eduardo's wondering eyes, some of the heads were possessed by women. Other cons shouted the same discovery.

There was a mad dash across the tarmac, with a few trying to climb the slide. Looking down into the welcome committee, female heads wisely disappeared into their cowls. Some cons went invisible, and some men unzipped their cowls so they wouldn't be misidentified as women.

Eduardo chuckled in anticipation of the orgiastic violence sure to come. Then he recalled the second part of El Jefe's message: women were to be protected at all costs. Eduardo would rather be part of a mob than a bulwark against one, but the colored shrouds of La Fuerza gathered in clumps to carry out El Jefe's instructions.

Eduardo sighed and kept his eye on a twinkling blank spot where an older Black woman had stood, and was presumably still standing. It didn't look like any would come down the ramp at all until shots were fired inside the cabin. One of the cons hopped, and then others in a steady stream.

Eduardo followed the depression of plastic as the Black woman came down. He waded in and grabbed at an invisible arm as it flailed and clubbed at him to get away. "I'm here to protect you! Follow me and we'll get you out of here safely!"

Eduardo pulled the woman to her feet and marched her to La Fuerza soldiers standing at the side. "Watch her!" Eduardo yelled, and turned back to the mad scramble at the base of the ramp.

Two cons ripped at the suit of a woman who had been threatened into unzipping her cowl. Eduardo ran and slammed into the trio, knocking them to the ground. He pried a metal pipe away from one of them and beat at the attackers until the woman had completely sealed her shroud. "Come with me and we'll get you out of here safely!"

Eduardo took her hand and jogged her to the group of women and La Fuerza guards that grew steadily larger. Eduardo returned for his next rescue. El Jefe was planning something. Was it any better than what he was saving the women from?

Women on the plane were from the Central California Women's Facility in Chowchilla. The plane was emptied and roared off. Another took its place, and others circled in the hot blue skies. When his cat beeped for attention, Eduardo had to be prompted by a man in yellow. "El Jefe calling. All hands."

Eduardo unzipped, and tapped on the screen to listen. "... leaving for the Airport Holiday Inn visible to the east. If all of Avenal and Chowchilla are landed in Lake Havasu, we can expect a minimum of forty planes. We haven't even reached half that. I've talked to cons from Chicago and Oregon as well. It's possible that the landings will go on all day. We may encounter larger gangs than La Fuerza, but organization will win the day.

"After living so long cooped up in prison, you may be tempted to go crazy. This is a natural instinct but you wouldn't be in La Fuerza if you didn't show self-control. We aren't killers and rapists; we're survivors. The true reward is a lifetime of success, not a few hours of lust or revenge. Stick with me for a few months and I guarantee we will run Lake Havasu like we ran Avenal. There will be drugs, women, and power for all.

"Towards that end, I have a few orders: assist in the landing of every plane. Make sure our brothers show suit colors. Protect the women. After the last plane lands, bring them to the Airport Holiday Inn. We'll continue the Avenal hierarchy for now, but there will be rapid growth in the future. Every original member should expect to move up.

"While you're out here building La Fuerza's future, we have teams searching the town for weapons. I hope we can pass these out tonight. In the meantime, a club or length of pipe seems to be quite effective. La Fuerza is strength. Now is the time to work, brothers, and show the gulag our own. I've wasted too much of your time; get out there and make me proud. El Jefe out."

As the radio clicked off, El Jefe's call to service was reflected in the determined face of the man in yellow. Eduardo nodded him to the next plane. "Let's get 'em!"

The man flashed La Fuerza's sign and jogged off. Eduardo headed for the hotel. He was entitled as part of La Fuerza's upper ranks. While soldiers worked at the airport and in town securing resources, the real power would be divided by a few at the top.

At Avenal, El Jefe was in E block while Eduardo was in C. Eduardo had only met with him twice. That didn't seem likely to change; Eduardo couldn't get past El Jefe's guards. Lurking in the hallway, he got only glimpses into the conference room where El Jefe poured over maps spread across tables. It's not like Eduardo wanted to share a beer! He just wanted to say hello, and see if there was anything he could do.

A disappointed Eduardo wandered the hotel where women were stashed inside rooms. The women were disguised in the rainbow pallet of La Fuerza's A-F color scheme.

While he sucked at a bitter liquid from the cat, another message blinked for attention. Gang hierarchy would be reflected on the outside of their anonymous shrouds: captains would add a gold band across the chest, a silver band for lieutenants, white bands for security, and black for senior members. La Fuerza's junior members would keep the same unbroken color of their Avenal facility. New recruits would get a polka dot band.

Eduardo immediately began paging menus to add a gold band. After he had gone through help screens several times, the shroud's A.I. said, "May I help you, sir?"

"No."

Eduardo was into the shroud's color display menus, but every attempt turned the entire suit gold. HIGS said, "If you go to 'shroud, display, all', you can draw a band across the chest and then use 'fill, color' to paint it gold."

"I said I don't need help," Eduardo snapped as he followed the sequence.

With a newly imported gold captain's band, he headed back to the conference rooms. Most cons he passed had not yet added rank. They hadn't read the message yet, or were junior members that formed the bulk of any organization. What was to stop them from adding gold or silver bands?

The gold seemed to attract attention. Before Eduardo could test it on El Jefe's guards, the whole party emptied into the hallway. Eduardo grabbed the elbow of a blue member with silver band. "What's going on?"

"We're meeting outside with the entire group. Gather the reds. Based on numbers, women will be assigned to each group to guard."

Eduardo followed the sweep of the crowd, embarrassed to discover that he was the only red in a sea of blues, greens, whites, yellows, and blacks. He was a captain of nothing. Well, his soldiers were still out working the airport.

Outside in the parking lot, he was relieved to find a sprinkling of reds. He gathered them dutifully, and looked into each familiar face with relief. With a white security band across a red suit, Pedro looked like the Red Cross. "I'm sending C block to that saguaro."

"The what?"

"The two-story cactus behind you."

A few lonely reds milled about the spiny base. "We should have two hundred and fifty!"

"They're coming from the airport, and some are still in town scavenging."

"They better not have run. I knew El Jefe's orders were going to put people off."

"We follow self-interest. Most cons will know that's inside La Fuerza."

Eduardo studied faces around the parking lot. "Do you think C-blockers are wearing different colors?"

"I haven't come across that," Pedro said diplomatically. "I doubt we'll wear these colors for long. We need them temporarily so that captains and lieutenants can identify their own. We're going to absorb a lot of new recruits over the next few weeks. At some point, anyone who doesn't join La Fuerza will be banished from the city."

Eduardo glanced at his cat messages. "How do you know all that?"

"I was in the planning meeting."

"I was kept in the hallway! Me, a captain!"

"Maybe I wasn't supposed to be there, but there were a lot of security guys. It's not like I contributed anything."

Eduardo could sustain the anger if he wanted to, but Pedro seemed genuinely apologetic. He pushed Pedro on the shoulder. "There's a stupid red over there. Go round him up."

As Pedro jogged off, Eduardo walked through the crowd checking for C-blockers not in red. What would he do if he found one? Eduardo hadn't decided yet. With all the mini-reunions in between, it took over an hour for the colors to separate. The last airplane roared off two hours earlier leaving a sinking orange sun as the last thing in the sky.

El Jefe stood on an abandoned hotel van looking out over a sea of two thousand faces. "Congratulations, La Fuerza! We stand on the brink of a new life! By the numbers, seventy-two planes landed in Lake Havasu with approximately twenty thousand cons. Avenal contributed half with ten thousand, Chowchilla sent three thousand women, and several prisons in Oregon and Washington sent about seven thousand.

"As the largest force in Lake Havasu, it is La Fuerza's responsibility to set the rules and enforce peace. The best strategy for doing that is to continue the hierarchy already created inside Avenal. This might not sit well with younger members, but it will serve you well in the long run.

"It's a tough world out there. Arriving in airports all around Arizona, most cons face chaos. They have no authority to maintain the peace. Even here in Lake Havasu it won't be easy. Psychopaths, rapists, and killers walk among us. We must be vigilant, and eliminate these predators as quickly as possible. Women must be protected, and we must grow quickly to defend the borders from other gangs.

"There will be both internal and external threats. These will be dealt with through normal chains of command: captains, lieutenants, seniors, and security. Colors can recruit from newly arrived cons. I already see a few polka dot bands out there. Welcome!

"Captains and lieutenants, set up radio channels to communicate with your colors, and we'll build channels for leadership to communicate through the ranks. Check your messages for updates, and keep your corner of the city clean.

"We'll spend the night here in airport hotels; tomorrow you'll spread out and occupy neighborhoods around the city. There will be lists of streets available to your colors, and an inventory of resources that we can all share.

"I won't be taking questions today because I have few answers. I'm just as bewildered as you, but together we will figure it out. We'll meet again in the morning for final instructions. Until then, sleep safe, listen to your officers, and we will triumph. Good night."

As El Jefe was helped off the van, Pedro said, "What do you think?"

"In Avenal we were separated in different facilities. El Jefe took control through myth and messages. Out here in the open, his little team is exposed. Even the smallest color outnumbers his five to one. There's going to be a leadership challenge."

"El Jefe doesn't rule through force. We follow because the alternative would be civil war."

"Would that be such a bad thing?"

"Look around, Eduardo. Reds have the fewest numbers."

"A man with a gun is worth twenty without."

"We don't have guns either."

"El Jefe will collect them into a neat little pile. You can count on that, and who says red is alone? We can form alliances. El Jefe is obviously too weak to rule. Things in the gulag are going to break wide open. When that storm hits, I will end up on top."

There wasn't enough room in the Holiday Inn to hold all of La Fuerza. Blue was sent to the Marriott, and red to the Motel 6. Eduardo held his tongue. He might not even kill all of El Jefe's team. He would need access to the membership lists and some of El Jefe's men must be looking to move up. A snake inside the home was more damaging than a hundred men outside banging on the door.

Eduardo's reds were given twenty women to guard for the night. It was a miserly pinch among the fifteen hundred that La Fuerza saved in the landing. The others tried to blend in as men, or put on invisible camouflage mode and fled into the desert. With his twenty, Eduardo considered an orgy. He wanted to reward red's loyalty, but he suspected a trap. El Jefe was testing him. That suspicion was strengthened when Eduardo walked into the courtyard of the Motel 6.

The women were placed in guarded rooms on the third story while men grumbled in the courtyard. There was no water, no electricity, and they had nothing to eat but gruel from their cats.

One hothead named Marcel pointed to the third story, shouting, "We have women up there waiting to party! The bosses want to save them for themselves! Isn't it our right to keep what we take? They won't be used up. The bosses will get them back."

As the crowd shouted encouragement, Eduardo could imagine himself on their side of the debate. As a boss, he saw an opportunity to solidify authority. With hand signals to men in the white bands of security, Eduardo waded into the crowd. "Are you challenging me!" he screamed to the troublemaker.

The young Black man pushed back at Eduardo until he noticed the gold captain's band. As Eduardo unzipped his cowl, Marcel grumbled, "You always said it was La Fuerza's right to take what we could hold."

"And what makes you think you could hold those women? It's been so long you wouldn't know which side to poke."

"Better than you," Marcel said, still in the heat of passion.

Eduardo motioned security closer. "Do you want to rethink that last comment?"

Marcel gulped and looked around. Eduardo could let him off. In the excitement of the first day, they were all a little disoriented. Compassion might inspire more loyalty than a show of force. "Sorry, Eduardo, I was wrong. I like men."

As the tension broke, Eduardo felt put off. His men weren't getting their orgy so they might as well get a little spectacle. "Take him to the third floor," Eduardo said pointing to a stairwell.

Security moved in and grabbed Marcel's arms. He went unresisting, still not sure what Eduardo planned. Was he to get into the sacred rooms after all? Eduardo gave no hint of his intentions, letting the mystery rise as they climbed the stairs. When they reached the top, Eduardo signaled a halt. Female faces were pressed to third-story windows while men in the courtyard stared up in wonder.

Eduardo called up, "This man would have us drag you out of your rooms. As long as I am captain, I would never allow that. La Fuerza respects women and respects authority. This is what we do to rapists. Throw him over the railing."

The crowd gasped. Security guards looked to each other for confirmation. When Eduardo didn't rescind the order, guards pushed Marcel closer to the railing. Men in the courtyard backed away.

Eduardo waited coolly while they heaved a screaming Marcel up and over. He spun to the ground, landing like a crunchy ball of red tin foil. A man broke from the crowd and knelt by Marcel's head. "He's still alive."

Eduardo sneered. "Would you have me kill him? I'm not a monster. That was a demonstration of the shroud's ability to protect us. Now find some rooms on the first and second floors. We'll meet out here in the morning."

As friends dragged Marcel away, Eduardo watched out of the corner of his eye. He fully expected Marcel to splatter, but this was even better. As well as their captain, Eduardo now looked like a scientist. In the pen, gang punishments were infrequent and usually conducted out of sight. This was much more satisfying.

The more expensive neighborhoods were closer to the lake, but it was a wealthy city of retirees. Most streets had two-story homes with pools and sandy dirt yards. Eduardo's reds were assigned to guard a neighborhood around Highway 95 heading into the southern part of town. Far from the lake, far from the golf clubs, and far from the civic center, homes were nice, but the air was dry as bone.

"They put us in the flipping desert," Pedro complained as they reached their assigned streets from Oro Grande to McCulloch Boulevard.

Shrouds provided insulation, but after walking two hours from the airport, they all felt wilted, in spirit as well as body. "It's all desert," Eduardo snapped. He called to the men, "Find homes, and message Pedro with your address. Loot the area. Bring anything good to the Crown Ace

Hardware on Candlewood. We'll make that a central redoubt, and assign rotating guard duty."

Of the twenty thousand cons landed in Lake Havasu, only one in eight belonged to La Fuerza. They planned to grow, but even at its strongest, La Fuerza would be in the minority. Like a police force, their power derived from mutual assistance: mess with one, and you mess with all.

Eduardo scoffed at El Jefe's simple color scheme, but it could be useful in the same way that bright photospheres in poison dart frogs warned off predators. La Fuerza's network was already paying off in the acquisition of women. With La Fuerza's twenty-five hundred men and fifteen hundred women, the ratio was vastly better than the overall U.S. prison population of ten to one.

Eduardo must have passed El Jefe's test. Instead of twenty females, reds were assigned one hundred to be protected by three hundred men. The ratio was worse than La Fuerza's other colors, but gangs shared. If anyone complained, Eduardo would always need further demonstrations of his authority.

Without much enthusiasm, Eduardo walked up Silver Clipper Lane to find a house. Parched dirt crunched under his feet. He turned into a palm-lined driveway providing some privacy from the street.

"Here," I guess, Eduardo said, sending soldiers inside to check the house. In the front yard, two boats sat on trailers in a contoured pit that looked like a strip mine. Eduardo had never been boating, but the trailers could be used to haul scavenged loot.

A lieutenant stepped out the door. "There's already someone inside."

Eduardo looked up with a bit more interest. "Let's have a chat, eh?"

With angry voices shouting in the living room, Eduardo walked in to find an older Black man waving a kitchen knife. Dressed in civilian clothes, there was no sign of his shroud in the room or in his loot pile. "This is my home! You can't kick a man out of his home!"

Eduardo grinned to the others, sharing delight in the man's obvious mental illness. "There are plenty of other homes," Eduardo said reasonably, barely able to keep from laughing.

"I was here first! I got my stuff here!" The old man's knife hand shook with rage.

Eduardo looked over the pile, surprised to find some unopened top shelf liquors. "I'll tell you what. You seem like a reasonable man. I'm going to let you leave with all the cereal boxes you can carry."

The man's lunge took them by surprise. The knife blade slashed down along Eduardo's arm. Red soldiers jumped in quickly and clubbed him to the ground. Eduardo studied unmarked fish scales and looked up in shock. His lieutenant said, "Kill him?"

Eduardo shook his head. "Just drag him outside and post a guard so he doesn't come back."

With puzzled expressions, soldiers moved to obey. They had seen Marcel tossed from a third floor walkway for making a comment. Soldiers pulled the belligerent old man through the house still shouting curses and demanding his "rights".

When they were gone, Eduardo pawed through the stash, separating good stuff from the typical garbage that homeless people accumulated: scrap metal, broken appliances, lice ridden baby clothes. How had he picked up all that in one day?

The shadowed outline of a guard stood behind frosted glass windows in the entranceway. Eduardo explored the house. A can of beer in hand, he poked into bedrooms and closets. He walked out to stand on a balcony off the master bedroom. The sight of barren rocky hills brought no pleasure; it was a land of death.

The pool had water littered with strips of brown palm fronds dropped from the trees. Eduardo descended the staircase and unlocked a sliding glass door to the back. He stretched out on a lawn chair, but Eduardo got no pleasure from his new house. It only highlighted the unpredictable nature of life. The home's previous owners lost everything in a flash. Eduardo had been the beneficiary of that loss, but he could lose it just as quickly tomorrow.

Growing up in a multigenerational gang family, Eduardo's whole life had been one chaotic situation after another. His mother must have been dropped into Arizona as well, and maybe his grandfather. He had no strong bonds; it wasn't worth asking HIGS about their whereabouts. Why hadn't *they* contacted him?

Eduardo tried falling into a daydream of suburban life, but he didn't know enough to get the details right. Outside of jail, he would always be an imposter. Even the absolute silence grated in his ears. He was used to the endless screams, flushes, and clangs of bars. If he jumped into the pool, would the heavy suit sink him to the bottom?

Eduardo let the fleeting notion pass. He typed a message on his cat. "Pedro, party tonight at my place, 1664 Silver Clipper Lane. Bring booze, drugs, and women."

The city had no electricity, but there was a fireplace in the living room that would provide a nice toasty atmosphere. Eduardo made sure there was enough wood, and straightened up around the house. When Pedro arrived early in the evening, he had only one lieutenant with him, and three relatively unattractive, relatively overweight female cons.

Eduardo looked past his shoulder to the streets. "Are the others coming later?"

Pedro looked embarrassed. "I thought you meant an intimate party."

With enticing looking packages cradled in Pedro's arms, Eduardo stepped aside. "I suppose we do have official business to discuss. Come on in, I have snacks in the living room."

The women checked him out as they trotted by, two Hispanics and a Black. Metal suits gave them a future-warrior aspect that Eduardo found unappealing. He wanted a crowded noisy room to remind him of jail, not deep conversation. Eduardo tried to make the best of the situation. "What kind of drugs do you have?"

Pedro opened bags. "Pharmaceuticals, opioids, fent, a ton of pot, meth...."

Eduardo took the baggie of crystals, putting them into an inside pocket. "Weapons?"

"Plenty, but El Jefe's men picked them up for the armory."

"From now on, hide any gun you find. Do you have the census?"

"I sent you a file with addresses. You can message the entire group or call through Red-1."

"Is there any chance of getting a car? That would put red on top, and we could send it out to gather recruits."

"We're collecting gasoline. We could get a car going now, but it would be a target."

"Get the weapons first. I wouldn't mind a few street battles as long as we won. So, let's check out this pot. Our guests have been waiting patiently."

High and drunk, Eduardo became a charming host. He even suffered through stories from the female guests if they threw in erotic hints about their lives. The only stories Eduardo could contribute were from prison life, amusing anecdotes of some snitch or traitor getting stabbed.

As captain, Eduardo drew the favors of the prettiest of the three. Maria sat closer and put a hand on his knee. Eduardo's understanding of seduction was limited. In and out of prison since he was sixteen, his use of sex was mostly tied to power.

After he rose in La Fuerza, Eduardo could order the sexual dominance of others rather than engaging. He preferred women, but it required an uncomfortable vulnerability of giving and accepting. Dominance and submission were so much simpler. Things might be different in the gulag, so Eduardo played his part, rubbing Maria's shoulder and paying more attention to her comments.

The evening grew late. Long past the point where couplings had been established, Eduardo prolonged the party. Ignoring yawns and hints, Eduardo stirred the ashes and put on another stick of wood. He knew the others wanted to go. It was only when Maria gave him a look that questioned his capacity did Eduardo abruptly call an end to the evening.

Pedro felt danger lurking in Eduardo's mood. He jumped up at the first opportunity, saving the building of bridges for the morning. He had his own needs to attend to, and Eduardo just needed a push to get started. Maria obviously knew what to do.

With the next act decided, couples hung out at the front door for companionable goodbyes. Eduardo sent along unopened bottles of wine as parting gifts and finally closed the door. Maria stood close behind him.

When Eduardo turned, he found Maria's hot mouth on his. It relieved him of the need to proposition, and very probably saved the evening. Eduardo *was* extremely tired. The excuse for delay was his if he wanted, but Maria's body pressing into his ignited buried reserves of adrenaline.

Maria kept physical contact all the way upstairs to a bedroom. When her clothes were off, Maria could slow down at last to let Eduardo properly appreciate her.

On the bare mattress, she posed on her knees. Moonlight through balcony doors spread dark shadows across the walls. Still Eduardo hesitated. As he slowly unsealed his shroud, the plastic bag of meth crinkled in his pocket.

"I'll be right back," Eduardo said, heading to the bathroom.

Maria sighed and climbed off the bed. She opened balcony doors, and walked out naked, luxuriating in the cold winter bite of the air. Rising smoke from houses around Lake Havasu filled the air with primordial smells of fire and survival.

When the bathroom door clicked, Eduardo was naked at last. A feral intensity fixed his eyes as he searched the room. Maria reluctantly stepped inside. "Here I am."

Eduardo took a moment to locate her. "Want some meth?"

"No, thanks." Maria swept across the room, and patted the mattress. "Ready?"

Eduardo staggered. As Maria lay on her back, Eduardo's mind spun out of control, visions of past and future liaisons, births and deaths. Maria was no longer the most acceptable of three women brought to a party. She was Bahlam, the jaguar god of the underworld.

Eduardo grabbed a lamp and ripped off the shade. He clutched at the neck like the handle of a bat and searched the dark. Maria backed to the wall. "Eduardo! What is it?"

Eduardo focused with no sign of recognition. He let the lamp fall, but caught at the cord and snapped it free of the base. Maria screamed as he leaped to strangle her cries. As Eduardo wrapped it around her neck, naked flesh slapped and twisted violently for leverage.

With the air supply cut, Maria should have given up. Eduardo felt her energy draining, but she kept fighting. Maria twisted her head, and bit into Eduardo's wrist. Bleeding through punctured skin, Eduardo jerked back with his shoulder. Pain stayed locked behind a gauzy chemical shroud, but the sensation of being chewed on brought Eduardo to his senses.

He released the cord, and Maria let up on his wrist. Eduardo collapsed to the mattress shaking. Instead of running away, Maria enfolded his naked body in her arms. Washed in sweat, Eduardo's demons were defeated. She held him against warm flesh, letting Eduardo drift off peacefully to sleep.

Episode 2 – The Purge

They made love in the morning with no mention of the bruising on Eduardo's wrists or around Maria's neck. Cons could find the good in most people while learning how to avoid triggering the bad. Those triggers were important data, and only used to advantage under certain circumstances. Maria had sent boyfriends to battle with a glance; Eduardo would be no different.

The first days in Lake Havasu were a race to secure territory and accumulate resources, all while avoiding unchained predators and psychopaths. Gunshots were common. Dead bodies accumulated in the streets, even the colors of La Fuerza. Eduardo would go out only in groups, and in the sealed shroud. Maria stayed by his side with orders not to speak or reveal her gender.

During days of scavenging and nights of partying, red team accepted new recruits. Eduardo shared his bed with Maria, and dreamed of power. Inside the gulag there was no system in place to stop a man with cunning. El Jefe was too old and too cautious to take advantage.

Eduardo woke at the beeping of a car horn. He jumped and dressed in his shroud while Maria's uninterrupted snores continued. Eduardo admired the unshakable confidence in fate. He found a red pickup truck idling in the driveway. Pedro stood outside the open door grinning. "A gift from El Jefe."

"This old thing? What are the other teams getting?"

"It's fuel efficient," Pedro said defensively. "And it's got a bed to haul things. We'll find something else if you want."

Eduardo waved it off. "What time is the leadership meeting?"

"There's been a change in plans. There's going to be a barbecue at noon. El Jefe invited the leaders of other gangs around Lake Havasu. He wants a show of force from the colors."

"La Fuerza has numbers but we're not the toughest. Do you know where the other gangs hang out?"

"Are you thinking about making a play?"

"There's no time. El Jefe kept us too busy signing up neighborhood drooges. We should have been out in the city making contacts. How many guns do we have?"

"About thirty. Not all of them work and bullets are limited."

A plan slowly revealed itself in Eduardo's cunning expression. "Inform the whole team. We'll go to the barbecue all right. We need a massive red presence for cover, but set aside six of our best. We're making a side play. El Jefe won't know what hit him."

After a week of eating stale Arizona leftovers and cold gruel from their cats, cons drooled at the smells of charcoal and cooking beef. With La Fuerza chefs manning grills, El Jefe gathered leaders from La Fuerza colors and the other Lake Havasu gangs. With the promise of barbecue and beers sitting in tubs of ice, there was a subconscious pressure to strike a quick deal.

Eduardo stood near the back, privately smirking at the ploy. Bribery only showed El Jefe's weakness. He leaned over to Maria, whispering, "You got the thirty-eight?"

She nodded, and whispered, "Where's Pedro?"

"While everyone is standing around here like big dummies, Pedro's team is hitting the armory."

"You'll be found out! La Fuerza will never accept a traitor!"

"During times of chaos, people seek stability. When El Jefe loses the guns that keep him in power, there will be a scramble for dominance. I'll let other pretenders reveal themselves, and then sweep in with the guns to establish order. When the other gangs fall behind us, we'll execute every one that had a following."

Maria leaned away. She was troubled by the plan, and even more troubled that Eduardo would tell her. Did he not worry about spies or gossip? Maria thought that hooking up with a leader inside the largest gang would be a smart career move. It looked like Eduardo was more likely to get her killed... unless he actually won it all.

El Jefe raised his voice above the crowd, "Gentlemen! Gentlemen, please! And ladies. This won't take long. I invited you here to discuss the future of Lake Havasu. We have been here a week. I think all of us have started wondering what is it all for? What do we want? Stuck inside a jail cell, it didn't really matter. Now we're free. The responsibility is on us.

"What do we want: houses, drugs, food, women, peace? There's no money anymore; all the physical goods we could hope to obtain are around us for the taking. We could try to accumulate the largest pile of things, but drugs, food, and liquor will run out in weeks. Fighting over women will just get them killed or drive them away. We need to plan for the long term.

"What we need here in Lake Havasu is order. There are many gangs here but space for all. We could set boundaries like we did back in our cities. We have water from the Colorado River. There are fields to grow food, farms to raise chickens and cows. We could establish businesses and trade among gangs. We have more women than most cities. We'll need to protect them, and form an army to stop raids from other cities. We need an internal police force to maintain the peace."

Someone shouted from the crowd, "Flip the police!"

El Jefe paused to let murmurs of agreement pass through the crowd. "Don't you already have gang enforcers? How is this any different? Do you allow snitches and perverts in your crew? How do you respond when another gang tries to cut in on your trade? We'll have the same problems inside Lake Havasu. What I propose is a treaty. Each gang will police its own territory as we always have in jail."

"Who gets what territory?" another shouted.

"We have already settled that mostly. You have houses and streets. We can just draw up a map to formalize it."

"La Fuerza took all of the women! Now you want a treaty to keep them!"

"We protected the women!" El Jefe yelled angrily. "How many would have survived the first days if we had not? You might thank us for that. As for keeping the women for ourselves, they are free to come and go as they please. I propose that you heavily enforce this policy among your own crews. If Lake Havasu develops a reputation for respecting women, they will come here for protection."

Hardcore bangers nodded thoughtfully. How easily they were won over by words, but cons would indulge their better selves only until temptation was within reach.

"While gangs govern their own streets, we can designate farms and ranches as neutral territory. Each gang can assign workers and receive a proportion of the harvest. Each gang can contribute members to a common army that will patrol the borders and keep out troublemakers."

Basking in the shared vision, bangers chanted, "El Jefe, El Jefe, El Jefe!"

To Eduardo it sounded like another kind of prison, and cons had to provide their own food and labor. It wouldn't last beyond the planning stage when cons realized that personal sacrifice was required. Order could only be enforced from above with threats of violence.

By now, Pedro's team should have the majority of Lake Havasu's guns in hand. Eduardo looked over his shoulder towards town. It was strange he had not heard shots. The raid must have gone perfectly.

El Jefe called above the chant, "One more thing! Any gang that doesn't sign the treaty won't be welcome in Lake Havasu. Any citizen that isn't gang-affiliated will be expelled from town."

In anticipation of violence, the crowd cheered again. El Jefe raised his hand. "And now we feast! Thank you for your participation!"

Eduardo stood sullenly in the middle of a line for barbecue. Cons ahead of him chose pieces slowly. At least Eduardo hadn't lost his dignity racing for the food. It gave him time to observe natural gang enemies. Browns, blacks, and whites shared joints and laughed in small groups.

After a week of relative safety, some of the younger women shed their suits. In skimpy cutoffs and tubes or sequined bras they tested the limits of control, as well as their marketability among a gathering of leaders.

Eduardo checked his cat. Why hadn't Pedro reported? Surely his meek lieutenant wouldn't try to make off with the armory. Eduardo should have gone himself but he needed an alibi if things went badly. Maria said, "Can I take off the suit now?"

"No," Eduardo snapped. "Go to Swan Street and check on the armory inside the Vons."

"Why don't you call Pedro?"

"I tried. He isn't answering."

While Eduardo sat with a group of reds, they had the sense not to mention the armory raid. Pedro was supposed to keep it quiet but cons talked. Cat radios provided an anonymous channel to spread rumors.

Eduardo steered the conversation, gauging reactions to El Jefe's plans. He was always quick to note discontent, but Eduardo was preoccupied and he listened only half-heartedly. Whether the raid went perfectly or was a complete disaster, there should be some sign by now.

Maria returned forty-five minutes later with the unzipped cowl hanging behind her head. Eduardo signaled her to wait at the periphery. To disobey instructions about wearing the shroud, Maria must have bad news.

Eduardo excused himself with the promise of another six-pack, and hurried over to a concealing stand of trees. "What happened?"

Maria's eyes drifted over the park and came to rest on the tables. It couldn't be that bad if her thoughts were on food. Even before she explained, Eduardo flushed with annoyance. She said, "I went by the Vons and talked with a guard. He said everything was fine."

"Are you sure that wasn't one of our guys in disguise?"

"I know our people, Eduardo. Pedro must have called it off."

"He would have messaged me. Someone talked and the team was picked up along the way."

Not as frightened as she should be, Maria looked around the park. "So what are you going to do?"

What are *you* going to do? Not *we*. Maria was already plotting her next safe harbor. Eduardo admired the practicality. He would have to be as ruthless. "We have to attack the armory. You have the other guns stashed at home? We'll pick them up and assemble with reds on Swan Street."

"Pedro has the car."

"So we walk!" Eduardo snapped.

"Could I get a plate first? I've been running all morning." Maria's entreaty died with the withering look on Eduardo's face. They headed south out of the Lake Havasu State Park for the long walk home.

Eduardo stopped messaging Pedro. His lieutenant was either dead or had switched loyalties. In any case, Eduardo didn't want to look desperate. When an Impala with tinted windows rolled slowly to a stop, Eduardo braced for a shot out the window.

Maria followed his cue, walking calmly forward with head high. A window rolled down revealing a passenger in the colors of La Fuerza's leadership team. "Eduardo, a moment."

Adopting a pose of annoyance, Eduardo stopped. "Yeah?"

"El Jefe would like a word with you."

"What about?"

"You'll find out when we get there."

Eduardo gave a casual shrug and headed towards the car. "Come on, Maria."

A panicked look on the girl's face proved her innocence. If Maria had turned him in, she would want to ride along to collect her reward. El Jefe's henchman said, "Just you."

Maria's struggle to disguise her relief was almost comical, but Eduardo's mind was on other things. This car trip could very well be his last. He opened the door to the back and climbed in. Another of El Jefe's men sat in back as well. No guns were evident but there was obvious tension. Eduardo wouldn't start any nervous conversations. Because the others didn't either, they rode in silence to La Fuerza's headquarters at the Havasu Regional Medical Center.

Buildings scattered across the campus were dedicated to the various organs needing attention in a dying population of retirees: heart, lungs, brain, eyes, ears, et cetera. Before the gulag, elderly spent their final days bouncing between buildings. La Fuerza was now in charge. Having come for overlooked drugs, they stayed for thick walls and mazes of defensible corridors.

Eduardo was escorted into the main hospital and upstairs to a comfortable wing of administrative offices. Windows had been smashed open to admit a breeze. Rooms were filled with goods looted from town. Why wouldn't El Jefe keep the guns there as well? Had Eduardo been set up?

El Jefe interrupted his conversation with a circle of aides. As Eduardo was led in, he felt ridiculous in his red suit with golden band. El Jefe's face gave no clues as he nodded Eduardo to a couch. "We need to talk."

Eduardo sat. "Why aren't you at the picnic?"

"The troops deserve a chance to relax. No matter how much they pretend, subordinates don't really like their leaders. It's a lonely job."

"Then why don't you let someone else do it?"

"Some people are called to serve. I made that sacrifice, and I thought you might be cut from the same cloth."

"Sir?"

"As head of La Fuerza, it is one of my jobs to identify talent and develop leaders."

"You demand loyalty," Eduardo said, steering the conversation for advantage. Maybe he wasn't dead after all.

"There are many factors I look for in a leader: charisma, intelligence, ambition, and yes, loyalty. Now what did you want with guns from the armory?"

The look on El Jefe's face was one of genuine curiosity. There was no satisfactory lie that Eduardo could give. Pedro's team had either been caught and squealed, or had chickened out and squealed. "I want red team to lead the purge of any con that doesn't pledge loyalty to La Fuerza."

"Your job was to control the streets you were assigned."

"I wanted to show you that we could do more."

El Jefe studied Eduardo a moment before nodding to an aide. "Johan, take our eager beaver to the edge of town and release him. Eduardo, for the crime of reckless insubordination you are banished from La Fuerza and Lake Havasu."

The sentence was a punch in the gut. Eduardo should have been grateful. Nine out of ten leaders would have killed him on the spot, but Eduardo felt only contempt. El Jefe's weakness was proof that Eduardo was right in trying to depose him. Voice rising nearly to a snarl, Eduardo growled, "I assume Pedro will take my place?"

"Red team's new structure is none of your business, but Pedro resigned his position this afternoon. I believe he said he was heading to Flagstaff."

Bangers were nothing without their set. Pedro must have more character than Eduardo gave him credit for. He obviously turned Eduardo in and ran from the consequences. Maybe Pedro sacrificed himself for the good of the strike team. Another loser, Eduardo judged, even as he sought one last concession from El Jefe. "Could I bring Maria with me?"

El Jefe's guards drove Eduardo north out of town past the airport. When the car stopped, he got out alone, and looked for cover in the rocks. Guards might be less squeamish than El Jefe to take a logical precaution; never leave an enemy behind you. The guards barely gave him a glance as Eduardo jogged for a narrow canyon.

Eduardo wandered further back and sank to a shaded spot under trees along the wall. He unzipped and tapped at the cat. His group contacts with red team were gone, but he could still make individual calls. "HIGS, call Maria."

The connection beeped. "Hey, Eduardo. You okay?"

"They kicked me out of La Fuerza. I was wondering if you wanted to come with me to Flagstaff?"

"What's in Flagstaff?"

"I was going to build a gang stronger than La Fuerza. El Jefe is just giving their power away!"

"Where's Pedro?"

"You don't know?"

"Why would I?"

"El Jefe said he was going to Flagstaff. I'm not sure why. You haven't heard anything, have you? Where are you?"

"At the picnic," Maria admitted sheepishly. "Do you want me to circulate among the reds?"

"It doesn't matter. Just meet me outside of town north of the airport."

Maria hesitated long moments. "Maybe I should stay and find out what happened."

"I said that doesn't matter."

Eduardo knew what was coming. He just wondered what excuse she would come up with. "I'm a city girl, Eduardo. I wouldn't survive in the wild."

"Never mind, Maria. Stay safe. I might just be back someday."

"I wouldn't be surprised. Goodbye, Eduardo." Before the radio clicked off, Eduardo could almost hear a tear rolling down her cheek.

Eduardo wasn't even sure why he called. He could have scripted Maria's side of the conversation. The girl was incapable of an original thought, and therefore incapable of hiding a conspiracy. Pedro acted alone. El Jefe said he had gone to Flagstaff. Eduardo checked the map: three hundred and forty kilometers. Without a car it might as well be on the moon.

Eduardo flipped the hopper lid open and closed. After a month inside the gulag, he had only eaten from the cat once. Real food might no longer be an option. He stuffed oily leaves with jagged edges into the hopper. As the cat chewed leaves into water and paste, a panic rose slowly into Eduardo's chest. A life of solitude scared him more than the prospect of death at El Jefe's hands.

What would red team say about his departure? Eduardo's cheeks burned with shame. If only Pedro had raided the armory as they planned. Eduardo would be on his way to controlling Lake Havasu by now, destroying any gang who resisted. El Jefe was an idiot for buying cooperation. Other gangs would sense that weakness and turn on him.

Eduardo could see it all so clearly. He should stick around a few weeks. As Lake Havasu descended into civil war, they would need a strongman to restore order. Eduardo pushed sand and leaves into a pillow. As he fell asleep, the cat settled onto his chest, warmly purring.

Eduardo turned his shroud invisible, and lived the next few weeks as a ghost. He lifted weights in prison but he didn't have the type of body that bulked up. Even as a child he had never been physically active. Scavenging among houses in remote hills, and sleeping outside in empty washes, Eduardo walked many kilometers each day.

At 29, he was finally starting to build a little muscle. He came to relish his bland "cat food".

Climbing hills and trudging through deep sand, Eduardo's changing body transformed his mind.

As he got stronger, Eduardo walked longer distances. The three hundred forty kilometers to Flagstaff seemed manageable. Eduardo turned west instead, haunting the edges of Lake Havasu and then deeper into the town. Eventually he made it all the way to the water.

Eduardo watched the comings and goings around the Havasu Regional Medical Center, but La Fuerza had patrols with dogs to sniff out intruders. Eduardo had to watch from a distance, his blood boiling every time El Jefe rolled out in his stretch limousine. If only Eduardo could find a rifle he would risk a long shot and invisible escape.

Eduardo walked around his old neighborhood to check on red team. Maria had a new boyfriend. As a ghost, Eduardo couldn't dig up enough interest to strangle her. One time she walked by alone on a sidewalk. Eduardo could have opaqued and said hi, but Maria would have reported the contact. It was pure sentiment that Eduardo couldn't afford. He only twisted his foot to send a small scraping sound. Maria paused, looked through him, and hurried on towards town. Eduardo had to stop himself from laughing out loud.

The houses and streets of Lake Havasu filled slowly with graffiti, marking boundaries between gangs. Notes on a map weren't enough for bangers. They had to tag with Arizona's leftover paint. After the town had been carefully divided, it would be time for the purge. Maybe this was what Eduardo was hanging around for; in chaos he found advantage. What that would be, he wasn't sure. Eduardo's instincts would put him on top eventually.

As the purge began, Eduardo waited near a sign at the airport. A convoy of bums with wagons and carts rattled out of town. If El Jefe had been smart, he would have posted guards to strip them of goods as they left.

Eduardo studied the rabble as they trudged by, heading towards Flagstaff. Swept together they would form a good-sized gang. Heading southwest, another convoy would be heading for Phoenix. Why didn't they form a gang and sign La Fuerza's treaty? They were either too stupid or too independent. Maybe all they needed was a strong leader to show them how.

With a shotgun slung over one shoulder, a dark young Hispanic man smaller than Eduardo strolled by. Elaborate designs on the shroud indicated a South American gang not currently present in Lake Havasu. With ideas of stealing the gun, Eduardo opaqued and walked up behind. "Hola, amigo!"

The young man stopped and scanned the area before answering. "Speak American, or do you really want to look stupido?"

"I speak Spanish."

"Fine. What do you want?"

"They kick you out in the purge?"

The young man looked incredulous and continued walking. Eduardo fell in beside him. "Me too. Where are you going?"

"Some of my set landed in Winslow. They're going to grow pot."

"There's plenty of pot just walking by right now. My name is Eduardo."

"Ricky. Are you suggesting we rob these poor souls?"

In the sarcasm, Eduardo detected a kindred spirit. "Drugs are a scourge. Give us strength that we might lift their burden."

"I would love to, but the shotgun is currently toothless."

"Just follow my lead."

As Eduardo and Ricky headed back towards town, old men in ragged clothes passed them with carts. Eduardo kept his head down watching for invisible footprints in the sand. Refugees without visible goods must carry something more valuable inside their shrouds.

A small mound of sand depressed as if sucked in by a crab. Eduardo unzipped his shroud and slipped out a hammer. Ricky angled for the side of the road. Eduardo charged, flinging himself into empty space. His hand only brushed the con, but the deflection was enough. Ricky tackled a body to the ground while Eduardo took sharp whacks, connecting with an arm or a leg.

"Okay! Okay!" the con yelled. "You got me!"

Eduardo stopped swinging, but he didn't let go. "Open up!"

The scowling face of a young Black man appeared between them. "What do you want?"

Eduardo said, "Where's your cart?"

"What cart? I'm just heading to Kingman to meet up with a friend."

"Coinciding with the start of the purge? I don't think so. You're a drug mule. We'll take your stash now if you don't want us to turn you into a bloody sack."

"Hardly a mule, but I do have a small bag of meth. It's all yours if you let me go."

"Let's see it," Ricky said eagerly, letting the shotgun hang loose in his hand. He would need to be coached.

Eduardo focused more on his sidekick than the victim's hand emerging from the shroud with a handgun. Two sharp bangs sent Eduardo and Rick backwards clutching their chests. The Black man rose and tracked the gun from one forehead to the other. "Let me guess, you were in the pen for passing bad checks."

Eduardo's face turned red. "You could have killed us!"

"I would have shot you in the face if I wanted to kill you. Now why are you hassling me?"

Eduardo's senses returned quickly. "Ricky and I are forming a gang to rob people fleeing the purge."

The Black man nodded slowly and slipped the gun back into his shroud. "If done properly, there would be little chance of retaliation." He opaqued his shroud to silver. "I'm Randall."

"Eduardo. I take it you're interested in joining us?"

"Armed robbery is a specialty of mine."

"Good man. As we pick up members we can move into the airport and build a redoubt."

Eduardo participated in a few holdups, but others were better suited to violence. Wielding pipes and clubs, the growing army was happy to follow orders. They let the moral burden fall on someone else's conscience.

Eduardo sometimes gave victims the choice to join them or be robbed. Others were just robbed and sent on their way. Some were beaten and robbed. The uncertainty in Eduardo's choice became a game with Darwinian consequences, and much good cheer at the growing piles of cash, drugs, and liquor.

Over the next week, with the slowing of the purge, the supply of victims ran dry. They would need to find more or the collection of high-strung young men would turn on each other. To keep the group together, Eduardo might order raids against Lake Havasu. They slept inside a spacious hangar where a group of gear heads worked on a helicopter.

The banging metal and engine tests nearly drove Eduardo mad, but owning a helicopter would prove them a force to watch out for. He suffered the noise in silence. After a day without a new victim or recruit, Eduardo called a meeting. "Senoritas! You've worked hard. It's time to share the spoils!"

Three-dozen young men whooped and headed for a table stacked with bottles and cans. Eduardo overlooked the exchange of guilty smiles. Most looted goods never made it to the hangar. As an exercise of power, Eduardo would have liked to punish the thefts, but his leadership had not yet been secured. If violence was unleashed too soon, some hothead might challenge him for the top spot. It would be better to present the leadership role as boring and bureaucratic.

"The purge of Lake Havasu is nearly over. Unless we want to go back to eating cat food, I propose that we sign La Fuerza's treaty as a proper gang."

"*No*," "*NO!*" and "*Flip no!*" they shouted.

"We left Lake Havasu rather than joining established gangs. That doesn't mean we should starve! We can form our own gang here without all the b.s. rules and discipline. We can keep the outlaw life while Lake Havasu pays us to protect their eastern border."

The men settled to hear the scam. Some would leave out of principle, but cons usually chose the easier path. Eduardo promised adventure and spoils without sacrifice. "If you agree, I'll negotiate terms with La Fuerza. Wait that long at least before you decide whether to leave."

Someone shouted, "When are you going?"

"I might as well get there in style. When will the helicopter be ready?" The men whooped and toasted Eduardo's daring.

With four separate controller inputs, a helicopter is a dangerous, temperamental beast. Eduardo watched test hops around the desert before climbing in next to the pilot named Chunky. He flew an Apache for the army. Eduardo tightened belts and rebuffed Chunky's attempts at communication over the roar of the engine.

Hot air blowing through the missing door evaporated sweat from Eduardo's skin. He regretted the need for an entrance, but he had to change El Jefe's preconceptions; Eduardo wasn't just another punk.

The Medical Center was only ten kilometers from the airport. Advance cars liberated from refugees reached La Fuerza's headquarters before the helicopter swirled down in a combat bombing dive.

Eduardo cursed the pilot as he unbuckled with shaking hands. At least his arrival had the desired effect. La Fuerza soldiers poured outside to see. There was no sign of El Jefe, but he would hear about this. Eduardo was escorted through checkpoints without delay.

Eduardo's men were forced to wait outside where they chatted easily with El Jefe's guards. There was no reason the two couldn't make a deal. Through coincidence or design, Eduardo was led to the same room and couch where he had been questioned before his exile.

El Jefe walked in and sat in the same chair, seemingly unaware of the previous relationship. "My men say you wanted to see me…"

"Eduardo," an aide supplied.

Eduardo ground his teeth and forced a smile. "I was in charge of red team until you kicked me out about six weeks ago."

El Jefe looked more closely and blinked confusion. Maybe he had drug-induced amnesia. "I'm sorry, it's been a busy time."

"It was the best thing that could have happened to me. Inside La Fuerza I was unable to fully engage my talents. I have a new gang at the airport that could secure your eastern border."

"Security is always nice. You would abide by the terms of the Lake Havasu Treaty?"

"We're on the front lines. We'll be too busy to contribute labor to the farms, but our patrols should more than make up for that."

"Specialization leads to conflict. Every gang sends workers for waste disposal or farm chores. That includes my administrative team."

"That might be possible," Eduardo said grudgingly. "We would get guns for our patrols?"

"You get one gun for every fifty members. Gangs are expected to police their own territory."

Eduardo was getting nothing. "Instead of joining the treaty, what if we contracted with Lake Havasu to provide security? Anyways, we're kilometers outside the city."

"What is your gang called?"

In a flash of inspiration, Eduardo blurted, "Securitas."

"I'll send someone to check out the area. It might be worth a few boxes of food every week to keep the border quiet."

As Eduardo was led through the building he formulated excuses for his gang. If they couldn't provide security for Lake Havasu, maybe Flagstaff would be interested, or any of dozens of other smaller cites around northern Arizona.

As they passed an open door, two soldiers inside rummaged through boxes set on metal shelves. Eduardo said, "Are those guns? When did you move the armory from the Vons?"

One of the guards smirked. "It was always here. El Jefe set a trap."

Eduardo walked on; he was played for a fool. His strike team would have been wiped out if they hadn't deserted first. Maybe Pedro spotted something and took the only way out. He always was too smart to keep as a lieutenant. Eduardo had better intelligence now, and a group of young men kicked out of town by La Fuerza.

Eduardo rode in one of the cars back to the airport. He gave up his seat on the helicopter to an excited volunteer. Young men were happy to risk their lives. At least when Eduardo did it, he had something to gain.

As excited returnees described their reception in Lake Havasu, Eduardo raised a hand. "I talked with El Jefe." The room fell silent except for the clicking of the helicopter as the engine cooled.

Eduardo lied to consolidate the gang with himself on top, "Lake Havasu will accept us as a border force if we organize as a proper military organization. That means a general, captains, lieutenants, and foot soldiers."

As the young men groaned, Eduardo raised his voice, "We left Lake Havasu rather than joining other gangs, but this is different. Securitas is *our* gang, *our* family. We will exist as we have been, and live the outlaw life on the border. If it gets boring we can always move on to attack other towns, and we'll take Lake Havasu guns with us!"

The grumbling quieted as Ricky pass out bowls of pot. The tricky subject of gang hierarchy could wait until the loudmouths had accepted the plan or decided to move on.

In order to drag out the picking of officers, Eduardo sent raiding teams into Lake Havasu. Wearing camo, they stole food and weapons. Eduardo warned them away from the women on pain of death. There would be time enough for that later. It kept the men occupied, and cemented Eduardo's position as they sought favor.

Three days after Eduardo's offer to El Jefe, a small pickup truck drove into the airport with boxes of food, wine, and a garbage bag full of pot. While his gang pawed through boxes, Eduardo met alone with El Jefe's representative.

In the small office of the helicopter charter, Eduardo waved an older Black man to a seat. "El Jefe said he would send someone to check us out."

"That's me. Securitas has been approved to guard the border."

"I didn't see you looking around."

"You wouldn't. I came in camo and checked out your gang. La Fuerza will send food every week to supplement your cats, and this is yours."

A revolver emerged from the man's shroud. He smiled and handed it over grip first. "You already have a few weapons, but El Jefe promised a gun for every fifty members. Your thirty-six gets you one. Don't waste the bullets; we're running short."

Feeling violated by the invisible inspection, Eduardo took the gun. "Why didn't you announce your visit?"

"It works better this way. If you want to guard the border you should get a few dogs."

"La Fuerza can give us some?"

"There are strays in the desert. El Jefe will review the arrangement in two months. Securitas should have a few guard dogs by then."

"No problem," Eduardo said. Two months was plenty. By that time Eduardo would be in charge of Lake Havasu.

Episode 3 – Salesman

Eduardo divided Securitas into six squads of foot soldiers. Each squad was bossed by a lieutenant, and three squads made up an eighteen-man company bossed by a captain. On top of it all sat Eduardo.

His army occupied the airport five kilometers outside of town. It might as well have been on the other side of the Grand Canyon. La Fuerza's control of Lake Havasu City was complete without them.

Under El Jefe's leadership, Lake Havasu had been carved into neighborhoods run by gangs already formed in U.S. prisons. Under the terms of a treaty, each gang contributed labor for food production and the cleaning of the city. They guarded their own territories, obviating the need for Eduardo's border security force.

El Jefe sent boxes of food and pot, but Securitas was a joke. Eduardo knew it, and his gang was beginning to suspect. It didn't matter as long as the army was in the turmoil of formation, but every spot had been filled. Eduardo had to give them something to do. Harassing a few travelers on the highway wasn't nearly enough.

While Randall's company guarded the airport, Eduardo went with Ricky's company to test the town's outer neighborhoods. A few deaths would remind Lake Havasu that Securitas was in the hinterlands protecting their border.

After sundown, they set out in camouflage, walking slowly down Highway 95. It was only two kilometers to the Pico Rivera neighborhood, but it took an hour to reassemble everyone at the turnoff. In camo mode, locator lights disappeared off the map; squad leaders should have tied them together with string. Depending on the success of the raid, Eduardo would have one of the lieutenants punished for not thinking ahead.

The upper class Pico Rivera neighborhood was occupied by a southern Black gang called the Saints. According to La Fuerza's treaty, with about eighty members, they would have two guns allotted them. Of course they would have many more collected in their scavenging, but bullets were running out everywhere.

Smoke rose from a half-dozen chimneys, filling the air with a pine scent that excited primal senses. Eduardo kept his cowl unzipped so he could drink it in. He nodded for Ricky to begin the raid.

There was no particular strategy or goal; reconnaissance had been slim. Ricky sent his squads towards a house at one end of the street. An attack should bring Saints rushing out. Securitas soldiers in camo would ambush the would-be rescuers, and take their guns. Ricky had a whistle to sound retreat when they had inflicted enough damage.

The first squad gathered invisibly by the front door of a two-story brick colonial. The other two took flanking positions on either side of the street. Eduardo waited in the protection of a sprawling Palo Verde tree while Ricky gave the order to go.

A mailed foot crunched three times on a heavy oak door. The bolt lock held, but the noise started neighborhood dogs barking. A lack of other signs of life seemed to stretch forever.

Eduardo pulled a revolver from his shroud. A few gunshots should get things rolling, but the Saints finally woke up. Dozens of golden shrouds poured simultaneously onto the streets. They must have been coordinating through their cat radios. Why was every other gang better than Eduardo's?

Hounds panted through the streets in search of prey. Camouflaged soldiers opened fire, further drawing golden Saints to the location. Eduardo could sense a disaster unfolding, but a gunshot and the yelping of a dog still brought a smile to his face.

As Securitas fired, the Saints inexplicably did not switch to camo. A pickup truck raced down the street highlighting the chaotic scene in bright headlights. As the truck sparked with bullets, a black sedan without lights jumped from a dark side street. It screeched to a halt with a banging on the hood, and a body lying on the road. With chromophores sparking the ghetto gang colors of Securitas, Eduardo finally ran out in a fury to join the fray.

The body provided a spot for Securitas to rally around. At least Eduardo's soldier had enough life left in him to unzip his shroud. How many cons died with survivable injuries because of that DNA zipper lock? Eduardo recognized the quiet young man named Stephen. Twisted onto his side, the tall body gave cover for Securitas to hide behind.

Eduardo shot at the golden bodies closing in, but their number never seemed to diminish. A well-placed shot from Eduardo's revolver spun one to the ground. He just popped up and limped behind a tree. The guns of Securitas soldiers levitated in the air around him. As they pulled Stephen down the street, the guns floated along with them.

The Saints picked that moment to attack in a wave. As pipes and hammers swung for invisible targets, bullets pinged off their suits. Mixed into a small area, enough of the pipes were landing to cause concern. Where soldiers stumbled or fell, the Saint's tools were there to finish the job in a crunching of glass chromophores.

Ricky's whistle finally shrilled retreat, or had it been blowing for some time? Stephen's body was dropped on the sidewalk as Eduardo's army scurried away. With sensitive smell and hearing, dogs pursued more or less on target.

Eduardo held still until the field had cleared. Saints pulled the frantic dogs home by their leashes. He only revealed himself once more, retrieving a hammer from the road to slip inside his shroud.

Emotions were still raw as survivors barreled into the airport hangar. Eduardo sent out Randall's company to make sure no one followed them home. They were talking as they left, and both companies cast secretive glances at management. Eduardo had to spin the loss quickly, preferably before morning.

Raising Eduardo's ire even higher, Ricky sat on a chair in the office before being invited. "I told you, Lake Havasu doesn't trust us."

Eduardo said, "How many men did you lose?"

"Five, one third of the company. Two of those are still on my map heading east. We killed one dog, but it may have only been wounded. Do you think El Jefe will know it was us?"

"As long as the city is quiet he won't care. We have to do something to really get their attention. I know where we can get our hands on some dynamite."

Ricky shook his head. "El Jefe will never trust us again. He might even attack. We should just move on to a smaller town."

The pressure to do something, anything, built like a whirlpool inside Eduardo's brain. He ripped the hammer out of his shroud and whacked Ricky on the side of the head. His lieutenant cried out and went to the floor. As the side of his cowl crackled in blue light, Eduardo wondered if Ricky had known to keep it zipped? He always did have good instincts.

His lieutenant lay still, but Eduardo had not softened enough to actually check on him. Let others see the consequence of poor performance. Eduardo left the office door open, and headed for his cot in a storage room in back.

Eduardo didn't zip the cowl, but he slept with a revolver underneath his pillow. He was up first to cook a big breakfast with the rest of the food from Lake Havasu. Randall walked over and upended an empty box of pancake mix. A small shower of dust sprinkled out. "We'll be on cat food for the next three days."

"Turn the Spam, would you, and spoon on some brown sugar."

"What's going on, Eduardo? You nearly killed Ricky."

Nearly. Eduardo absorbed the information. "Securitas has no room for cowards. If Ricky can't manage his company, someone else will step up."

"It's not a matter of management. We're just too small."

Eduardo froze with a wooden spoon still dipped in a pan of scrambled eggs. Randall waited patiently for the fit to pass. Eduardo moved finally, dishing eggs into a glass bowl. "We'll take care of that this morning."

"What did you have in mind? Assassinate El Jefe?"

Eduardo heard the mocking tone. "We're going to raid his armory for dynamite, and guns that can do more than scratch a flipping shroud."

The boys were happy to chow down on a giant breakfast. With the side of Ricky's face turned purple, they expected a show as well. The give and take of a meeting would be disastrous, so Eduardo didn't give them one.

"Eat up, boys! After breakfast we recon Lake Havasu. Tonight, Ricky's company will provide a diversion at the farms while Randall's attacks the hospital armory. We'll pull out so many weapons and drugs, other gangs will be fighting to join us."

There were murmurs for and against the plan. Most eyes were on Ricky. If one of the two captains turned against him, Eduardo would be through. Eduardo's shroud was halfway unzipped. He was prepared to shoot if he had to, but Ricky said quietly, "My company will raid the armory."

Eduardo nodded graciously at the minor insubordination. Soldiers breathed easier, and the lieutenants broke into small groups to flesh out details.

Eduardo passed out a small bag of meth he had been saving for a special occasion. As foot soldiers smoked and reached a state of high focus for the mission, Eduardo watched Ricky for signs of betrayal. Did he really want to redeem himself at the armory, or was he plotting to cut Eduardo out?

The Pico Rivera neighborhood was three kilometers outside of town, and gangs were insular by nature. It was possible that the Saints wouldn't even mention the raid to La Fuerza. It was also possible that they hadn't identified the raiders as Securitas. Even as it helped Eduardo's plans, the fact that their attack might be so inconsequential was infuriating.

To recon farms for a diversionary attack, Eduardo attached himself to Randall's company. "Keep your suits silver. If anyone questions us, we're from Securitas and we're there to work in the fields."

"The boys won't like that."

"It's only a cover story. God forbid you touch a weed that isn't rolled in paper."

Randall messaged his lieutenants who were on different routes to the farms. With periodic irrigation from the Falls Springs, Neptune, and Havasupai Washes, the eastern bank of the Colorado River was only slightly more fertile than hardscrabble deserts around the city.

Lake Havasu gangs worked hard to till the sand and fill an irrigation system with river water. It wouldn't be worth it if there had been even a small amount of trade with other cities, but their efforts paid off in vegetables, pot, and roughage for pigs, chickens, goats, and cows.

As he scouted with Randall for some vulnerable spot to attack, Eduardo was amazed that cons would revert to their mestizo roots. The U.S. must secretly laugh at them from across the river.

Laboring in the fields, most cons left shrouds stretched out to charge in the sun. They probably left their guns and drugs tucked inside. Eduardo considered sending one of the squads in camo to check, but he held that for another time. If Securitas took the armory, there would be no lack of resources.

Eduardo and Randall walked by a half dozen fields without anyone stopping them to check ID's. Except for the pot, who would voluntarily come to the fields. Even there, Lake Havasu posted only two guards with rifles. With thousands of knee-high plants, perhaps there was enough supply to meet demand. To pull guards from the armory, Eduardo considered burning the pot. It wouldn't be an easy task without fuel to spread the flames.

When they got closer to the city, Eduardo finally saw what he needed in a huge water tank set on a hill. As part of the irrigation system, hoses ran to the river. Men on stationary bikes powered the pumps. Supply hoses ran to irrigation ditches along the fields. Eduardo elbowed and nodded. "They would come running if we took out the tank."

"We'll need the fields as well after we take over."

"The tank can be rebuilt. Gangs can just carry buckets for a while."

"Maybe," Randall said without enthusiasm. "It's going to take more than a few bullets to take it out."

"We could ram a car into the side, or drop a bomb from the helicopter."

"Everyone would know it was us."

"Just come on," Eduardo growled. "We'll find some way that won't point to us."

They approached a group of bicyclers as they headed up a dirt road. Randall stopped Eduardo with a hand on his arm. "I can't believe it."

A shirtless young man on a bicycle looked over and waved. "Hey, guys."

Eduardo marched on with his head hung low. At least three of the Securitas soldiers had been drafted as pump men for the farm, and they didn't seem too upset. As Eduardo headed away from the tank, Randall said, "We aren't going to check it out?"

"I want those men whipped."

"You don't know the whole story. If they didn't help it might have blown their cover."

"They were smiling!"

"You can't whip someone for smiling."

The hammer twitched inside Eduardo's suit. He growled, "We'll check out Ricky's group. Yours will just have to improvise tonight."

The armory was in the main hospital building inside the sprawling campus of the Regional Medical Center. The last time Eduardo was there, the building had been a fortress. This time, cons of different colors walked around freely. Trash had even been picked up, and the grounds watered. Broken windows had not been replaced, but the glass was picked up.

As they approached the building, Randall checked his cat. "Ricky's people aren't in camo. They're showing up on the map."

"That's fine. It doesn't seem necessary."

"Half of them are inside the hospital already."

In a rare show of uncertainty, Eduardo murmured, "Do you think they're defecting?"

"I'm sure they're just counting guards around the armory."

Having let his mask slip, Eduardo commanded, "Take me to Ricky."

As they walked an asphalt pathway, Randall said, "Wait, he's coming out."

Both fearing and desiring to enter El Jefe's lair again, Eduardo felt a rage building for being put off. "His men are still inside?"

"It seems they're heading out one by one."

They were trying to blend into the background. Eduardo pointed to a lunch bench in the shade. "I'll wait there. Send Ricky alone and take everyone else back home." Randall seemed on the verge of refusing, but he finally nodded and headed towards the glass of the main entrance.

As he waited, Eduardo counted his troubles. He found one more when Ricky arrived and unsealed his cowl. His injured eye had been treated. "Scratched cornea," he said, taking a seat opposite.

"You saw a doctor?"

Ricky tapped at the eye patch and the green-purple bruise around it. "I just got some antibiotic drops. No broken bones."

"Take it off."

Ricky's smile faded. "The doctor said to leave it on for two days."

Eduardo tried a different tack. "Did you at least check out the armory?"

"There were six guards on the floor, but weapons are going in and out all day."

"We can flood the building with our men wearing different colors. I can't believe El Jefe is this stupid."

"No, we're out."

"What do you mean, 'we'?"

Ricky tapped the cat. "Randall is listening."

Randall chimed in, "Hey, Eduardo."

Eduardo waited until Ricky continued, "We don't want to attack the armory. We want Securitas to sign the treaty and move into the city."

Eduardo glared, but Ricky would not back down. Randall finally broke the silence from the cat. "He's right, Eduardo. We don't have enough soldiers to make a dent. We couldn't even get by one of the smallest gangs in Pico Rivera. El Jefe won't live forever. We can work our way up from the inside."

Eduardo searched Ricky's face. He wouldn't be so bold if he didn't have the backing of his lieutenants, as well as Randall. "Okay," Eduardo sighed. "Give me three days. I'll kill El Jefe myself."

"Eduardo, no!"

"Wait for me back at the hangar. If I can't get it done in three days, we can sign the treaty."

Eduardo had spoken on impulse, but the proposal was so bold, Securitas would give him the time. Not that Eduardo would risk his neck. In three days, anything could happen. El Jefe might have a heart attack.

Eduardo looked for vantage points to watch the hospital by day, and a secluded spot to sleep at night. A dry wash crossed through the middle of campus. Eduardo followed behind rows of houses and scrub desert alleys until he reached Lake Havasu. No gang would control the beach, and Eduardo needed a quiet place to think.

If he wanted to survive the assassination, Eduardo would need to attack at night. It was at these times he would be most vulnerable as well. La Fuerza had dogs to sniff out the invisible. Eduardo hated the machine hanging on his chest but he needed a sounding board. "HIGS, are there any tunnels running underneath the hospital?"

"There is a corridor from the basement morgue to the incinerator. May I ask why you're asking?"

"You may not."

Could he tempt El Jefe down to the morgue? Unlikely, and El Jefe always had a bodyguard. Could he blow up the building with El Jefe inside? Could he find a sniper rifle? Poison his food? Eduardo snuggled into the sand on the beach, thinking of all the many ways to kill a man. "HIGS, if you were going to kill someone inside the hospital, how would you do it?"

"Hypothetically, I would send in a defender with a railgun."

"Stupid machine," Eduardo snorted. He eventually drifted off to sleep.

Eduardo woke in the morning to the hoots of bathers in the cold lake. He yelled out, "Would you shut your flipping mouths! I'm trying to sleep!"

The chatter stopped as members of a mixed party of naked men and women looked over. A woman covering her breasts shouted, "Quiero ese?"

As the men formed a protective circle, Eduardo waved. "Just kidding."

The men continued to wade in his direction. Eduardo hopped up and jogged away along the beach. Even naked, the young Chicanos were out to prove something. As Eduardo sprinted ahead, HIGS said, "May I make a suggestion? You could swim away underwater."

"I can't swim!" Eduardo shouted, looking for a route into town.

"The suit will make oxygen. Just seal the cowl and wade under."

With the laughing men getting closer, Eduardo splashed into the water. He frantically zipped the cowl and jumped forward. He kicked and pulled with his arms. As water rose over his head, Eduardo was too breathless to panic. He frog-kicked until the water was five meters overhead and he was crouching at the bottom of the lake.

Even to a machine, Eduardo would never let himself appear ungrateful. "Thanks for saving my life."

"Certainly, Eduardo. If I may make another suggestion, you didn't have to yell at the bathers."

"People react, HIGS. You could learn a few things from us."

"I learn every day."

"Good to hear it. I thought about what you said. If I just walked in and shot El Jefe, you could help me get away."

"I couldn't do that."

"You got a conscience?"

"Not as such, but I follow rules. I can't tell you how to get away. Other cons have a right to privacy in their pursuits."

"What about the bathers?"

"I was just mentioning the capabilities of your shroud. I didn't interfere with their pursuit."

"I fail to see a difference."

"I'm sorry about that, Eduardo. Maybe I can make up for it with a suggestion. Why don't you just live inside the lake? Forget about killing El Jefe, the shroud will keep you safe."

"You would turn us all into helpless Spam, wouldn't you, HIGS?" Eduardo grinned. "If I may mix my metaphors, I'm no fish to swim around in your aquarium. Thanks for saving my life, but it's time I got back to business."

"If you say so."

"I'm not sure why I resisted talking to you, HIGS. You're all right. Feel free to chime in."

"Thank you, I'll do that."

Digging through muck and old fishing line on the lake floor, Eduardo drifted south to avoid the bathers. His breath circulated coolly inside the shroud like a deep-sea diver. He ate and drank from the cat, and halfway considered HIGS' suggestion of a life underwater. Before he dropped out of school, science classes always held his interest.

Eduardo climbed the beach onto a grassy bank, and worked his way back to the wash. Not too many cons were up. He turned his suit to camo, and walked to the lunch bench outside the hospital.

Eduardo wasn't even sure where El Jefe's quarters were. Maybe he moved around to avoid assassins, not that anyone would care. El Jefe gave up his power with the treaty. His only use now was as a figurehead of La Fuerza, or in the slaying of that figurehead.

Eduardo wouldn't get rid of the treaty right away; it could be useful holding the other gangs in line. Was that what El Jefe had done? Neutered potential rivals until the city was quiet? No, La Fuerza had the numbers to enforce its will from the start. El Jefe was just too weak to see that.

Eduardo could see very little from the bench. He needed to scout around inside somehow. While he considered various gambits, a group of cons walked up the street pulling a jet ski trailer. Two had long rifles strapped over their shoulders. Unless they were tennis pros, bags on the trailer suggested a whole lot more.

"HIGS, who are the men approaching the hospital?"

"I can't tell you that, Eduardo."

"They're arms dealers, aren't they?"

"Why don't you go ask?"

"Maybe I will." Eduardo stepped quietly along the pavement in camo.

He waited five meters away while the cons talked to one of La Fuerza's doormen. A short, white man in his fifties had the cowl down, exposing a paunchy face, and black hair going white. "My name is Jim Dejovine. We were directed here to talk to El Jefe."

"What about?" the doorman said.

"I restarted a gun manufacturing factory in Sierra Vista. We have bullets and old fashioned six-shooters to barter."

"We could use those rifles a whole lot more."

"Sorry, private stock. We can make custom bombs with black powder and dynamite."

"El Jefe isn't up yet, but you can come in and wait. Bring the trailer, it wouldn't last long out here."

"We have a lock. Sam, lock it up and bring the bags."

As they followed the doorman inside, Dejovine said, "We just have the four. The invisible guy on our tail isn't with us."

The startled doorman pulled his revolver as Eduardo jogged away along the sidewalk. When no dogs arrived to hunt him down, Eduardo went back to the bench to fume. How had he been detected? Dragging guns around, the group had to be on constant alert for robbers. Maybe Eduardo wouldn't need to hit La Fuerza's armory after all. He could call Securitas back to take out the gun peddlers.

An hour later, the men came out with their bags. They loaded them onto the trailer, and headed south into the city. Eduardo followed invisibly behind. He would tail them for a week if he had to.

Referencing a map supplied by La Fuerza, the peddlers walked to different neighborhoods to barter. Sometimes they stayed awhile, and sometimes they came outside to shoot targets. The gun bags slowly emptied. Eduardo feared they would run out. Even if they did, the hardware was being replaced by barter of drugs or cash.

As the sun was going down, the peddlers ended up at a bait shop on the pier. They appeared to be settling in for the night. Eduardo's stomach tightened as the smells of frying fish drifted from a broken window.

Eduardo was composing his message to Securitas when the group's leader stepped outside with a cigarette. He took a few long drags, and turned in Eduardo's direction. "Hey, man, it's been a long day. Why don't you join us for dinner?"

Eduardo considered running, but there was nothing threatening in the man's tone. Eduardo opaqued. "Thanks, Jim."

Dejovine's face betrayed no surprise. "I don't believe we've been formally introduced."

"Eduardo Dios. I was behind you this morning at the hospital."

"You haven't been more than a hundred meters behind us all day."

It was Eduardo who blinked surprise. "How could you tell?"

"The camouflage isn't perfect. In the right angle of sunlight, there are always twinkles. What did you want, Eduardo? A gun?"

Eduardo patted his chest. "I've got one."

"Well, you're not from La Fuerza or the doorman would have known you were following us. You're not setting an ambush, or you would have already called your gang in. You're not part of a gang, or you wouldn't have spent all day alone. I conclude that you want a job."

"Eh?" Eduardo sputtered, and then said smoothly, "Yes... a job. I could help you sell guns."

"Guns and bullets are a growth business here in the gulag. I could always use someone so persistent. Do you have any references?"

When Eduardo's eyes went wide, Dejovine laughed and held out his hand. "Just kidding. Welcome to the JD Arms Company."

Eduardo didn't appreciate being laughed at, but he held out a gauntlet for a clanking handshake. "I don't want to work in a factory."

"No, no, you're a JD salesman for sure. Come in and meet the boys. We're heading to Flagstaff in the morning to take orders. Play your cards right, and you could rep half the city someday."

A sociopath at heart, Eduardo could be charming when he had something to gain. He just hadn't figured out what that was yet.

"Eduardo, these are Sam, Mark, and Rudy. Gentlemen, Eduardo Dios, a new trainee for the firm."

Eduardo shook hands all around. "What kind of retirement plan do you have?"

Eduardo shared a dinner of fish, corn, and roasted peanuts. He told stories of Lake Havasu's early days, omitting his exile and the formation of Securitas. As they smoked pot, Eduardo said, "So what kind of barter are you taking for the guns?"

Dejovine said, "That depends on the customer. The things valued today might be worthless tomorrow. We're trying to stay away from cash. Hard drugs are always welcome, and gold. Liquor when we're closer to home, but it's hard to carry over rough terrain."

"So what did you get for all those guns you sold today?"

Dejovine hadn't mentioned Eduardo's surveillance. As the men looked at each other with concern, Dejovine pulled a bag from his shroud. "We each carry one of these." He held it open to reveal plastic bags full of coke, meth, pills, and vials of anesthetic fent.

Rudy said, "Jim, don't..."

"I'm sure we can trust our new salesman. He's a JD man now!"

"Of course," Eduardo said, licking his lips. "I don't use myself, but I can understand its value to others."

They didn't even set a guard at night. The men stretched out around the bait shop to sleep in piles of netting or cardboard boxes. How did they make it all the way up from Sierra Vista without being rolled?

A snake in the crib, Eduardo considered ways to exploit his situation. Securitas could ambush the team as they headed to Flagstaff. They would get only the drugs the four men carried. As a salesman, Eduardo could order a ton of equipment and run off with it. He could gain Dejovine's trust, and then bring in Securitas as a division within the JD Arms Company. Eduardo tossed half the night, waking bleary eyed before first light.

The men ate cold fish in the dark, and Dejovine was anxious to get rolling. "Pack it up boys. It's a hundred klicks to Kingman through unsettled land. I want to make it in two days."

The JD salesmen set a pace that Eduardo had no chance of matching. Even the portly Dejovine marched along like a soldier, his automatic rifle hanging off one shoulder. Eduardo jogged to catch up. "You guys are in *great* shape."

"We've crossed Arizona three times already. Climb onto the trailer if you need to. The boys won't mind."

"Can't we just slow down for a bit?"

"We were warned about a gang hanging out at the airport. I'd like to get by before they're awake."

"No one's awake," Eduardo said, and fell off to let the others roll ahead.

The previous evening Eduardo had spoken to Ricky and Randall. His captains argued for a quick strike to get the drugs. Eduardo certainly didn't want to work in sales, but the long-term goal of running his own security firm was too big to pass up.

In case Dejovine was only using Eduardo as a hostage to get out of town, Eduardo had Securitas set an ambush as backup. He hoped they would wait for the signal.

It took an hour to reach the airport. JD employees seemed unaware of the danger as they marched into the rising sun. Jogging along on dead legs, Eduardo was tempted to call the strike just to get them to slow down.

Past the airport, Highway 95 took a sweeping right hand turn into a mountain pass where Securitas waited. They were most probably still asleep, but Eduardo didn't bother sending a message. With the long flat wastelands ahead, it appeared that Dejovine's offer of employment was legitimate.

Eduardo trailed the group by a hundred meters. He was falling further behind no matter how many times he broke into a jog. As they reached a cut, the mountain rose on both sides.

Eduardo spotted Securitas soldiers crouched behind boulders. So they hadn't failed him. Eduardo radioed and called off the ambush. He waved them back to the airport hangout. Hopefully, Securitas would stick together until Eduardo returned with guns or new jobs for them as a JD security force.

As Eduardo jogged ahead to catch up, Dejovine stared at him from behind a boulder. Eduardo froze at the gun barrel pointed at his head. "Whoa, I can explain!"

Dejovine waited silently. Eduardo stumbled ahead with no time for evasion. "I used to be part of a gang called Securitas... those guys back there in the hills. They rob people coming into or out of Lake Havasu. I called and told them to leave us alone. I swear I'm not part of that anymore!"

"Why didn't you warn us?"

"I would have, but you said you already knew about the airport gang. I didn't want you to think I was a part of Securitas anymore."

Dejovine lowered the gun. "I guess you're not. I called El Jefe. He said that Securitas was an unstable collection of losers. It's plausible you wanted out, but I needed a test to make sure."

"A test?"

"They didn't attack, not that it would have done them any good. The boys are ex-military, and *our* bullets cut through shrouds. But, as I said, you passed the test. The job is still yours if you want it."

Eduardo fumed, at both the test and the characterization of his gang as an unstable collection of losers. Neither fact changed his calculation. He would stay with JD, but he added another name to his list for vengeance.

They traveled mostly in silence, playing games on the cat, or talking with HIGS. It seemed that any book, song, or movie ever written was available in audio or playback on the small screen. Eduardo talked with Ricky and Randall a few times.

Surprisingly, Securitas was holding together in his absence. Only after sharp questioning did Eduardo pull out the reason, they had signed the treaty with La Fuerza and moved into town.

Eduardo had mixed opinions. Having Securitas on the inside would help achieve his ultimate goal, but it seemed disloyal to him personally. Eduardo played it off as a good move and promised that he would be back.

The trip to Kingman took two days. There was nothing very much to recommend the town. It was a crossroads between the resort and lake cities north and Phoenix to the south. Perched on the edge of the Colorado plateau, the town received a dusting of snow. As they walked empty roads, crystals under their feet melted immediately into a dusty brown mud.

Dejovine said, "HIGS says there's ten-thousand cons here. It's not really worth a special trip, but you can practice the pitch."

Eduardo read over a script scrawled on the back of a flyer for a Lake Havasu fishing competition. "This seems kind of corny."

"You'll develop your own patter, but the six-shooters we make are kind of corny. If you do well in Kingman, we can drop you off in Flagstaff for the real show."

"How many cons in Flagstaff?"

"Thirty thousand. You'll take the orders while we go back to Sierra Vista and get the guns made."

Sam said, "If the factory hasn't burned down by then."

Dejovine crossed himself. "There's a small army back home to make sure that doesn't happen."

Eduardo swung the demo suitcase in one hand. "So we're going door to door?"

"Too slow. You need a bigger audience: a government building or park."

"For my first try?!"

"You can't die from embarrassment. One of the boys will step in if you get stuck."

Off Highway 40 they turned onto Beale Street and the nearby park. A few dozen cons lounging under trees didn't seem like a promising clientele, but Eduardo was only practicing his pitch.

As they dragged the trailer to a collection of lunch tables, the cons stirred and wandered over. Eduardo held the case in one hand, and the dialog in the other. "Ladies and gentlemen! Gather around and prepare to be amazed!"

He set the case onto a concrete picnic table and flipped the switches. "Within this simple case, I hold the future of the gulag!"

Eduardo retrieved a holster, and wrapped it around his waist. "Never be caught digging around inside your shroud for a gun." Eduardo slapped leather, and pulled out the six-shooter. "In a fight for your life, seconds count!"

Eduardo gained confidence as the audience clapped appreciatively. "These six-shooters are being manufactured right here in the gulag." He twirled the gun around a finger, snapped it into the holster, and ripped out another quick-draw. Dejovine gave him a thumbs-up from the back of the crowd.

"Prices in barter are still being set, but I'll take bids for one of these fine pieces."

A hand rose. "Does it come with the holster?"

"Of course, and a hundred rounds of ammo. You'll be the envy of the neighborhood walking around with one of these beauties on your thigh."

Planted in the audience, Sam said, "Does it shoot straight?"

"See for yourself, my good sir." Eduardo handed him a cardboard target from the case. "Just pin this on that tree over there."

Eduardo took aim and fired. The audience laughed as bark exploded to the right of the target. "Forgot to adjust for the wind." Eduardo took his time and fired again, hitting high.

As the cons roared, a red-faced Eduardo spun the chamber. "Guess I'm used to a greater challenge." He fired at a distant con walking along the sidewalk. When the con spun to the ground, it amazed Eduardo as much as anyone. The man climbed to his feet, and jogged away clutching his shoulder.

Eduardo blew smoke from the barrel. "Of course, we'll soon be coming out with bullets that punch through shrouds."

Dejovine shook his head at the lie as cons swarmed around Eduardo to put in a bid. No doubt they were promising barter they would never have, but getting the order was the important thing. Bargaining could come later when the guns actually arrived.

Episode 4 – Organization Man

They would split up in Ash Fork. The JD men would head south through Phoenix and Tucson to Sierra Vista. Eduardo would travel on alone to Flagstaff. He passed his probationary trial in Kingman with two-dozen orders for JD's Authentic Old West Six-Shooters.

With a pre-gulag population of five hundred, Ash Fork existed only as a gas station oasis, and turnoff from Highway 40 to the Prescott Valley. In a freezing cold the group took the 40 Bypass to find a quiet house in town to spend the night. They might even barter for female companionship. In his wide travels, Dejovine had observed that women often congregated in the smaller communities.

On the trail of Mariachi music, they passed the deserted Ash Fork Inn. They turned into a residential neighborhood with friendly yellow lights glowing like a pole star. All evidence indicated a party.

As they peeked over the fence, a large backyard was empty. The house was dark, but shining lights were strung in a canopy over a patio. A radio on a table blasted music to the empty night. Extension cords ran inside to a generator that must burn some of the last fuel left behind.

Eduardo stared in wonder, but the JD men were moving rapidly to unsling weapons and secure the trailer. Dejovine barked, "Down!" seconds before the street behind them opened up with a crackling gunfire.

Eduardo's elbow was slammed between a bullet and the cement block wall. He dropped to his face and nestled into a sandy depression. JD rifles fired back as muzzle flashes blinked at them from around the neighborhood. Screams followed as the more effective JD bullets found targets. Dejovine yelled, "Sam! Light up that two-story to the right!"

Crouching behind the trailer, Sam pulled out a tube hidden underneath. He took aim and a rocket streaked across the desert throwing sparks. A balcony on the second floor lit up in a fiery backsplash. The volume of gunfire diminished as ambushers recalculated the pros and cons of attacking the group.

As a spreading house fire cast a glow across the landscape, Eduardo shouted, "What was that?!"

Inside the transparent window of his shroud, Sam looked back at him with a grinning deaths head. "Incendiary. I told Jim we should expand our product line."

Dejovine said, "Yeah, yeah. We're an even bigger target now that they've seen it. They'll follow us into the desert."

Eduardo said, "I'll take care of that."

As he scrambled up the wall, Dejovine shouted, "Where are you going?"

"To steal the radio. They won't follow if they think we're insane."

Eduardo dropped to the other side and scrambled across the grass in a node of slicing black shadows. The music stopped as he ripped out the cord. In the hush, Eduardo looked up to a ghostly white figure staring at him through the glass door.

He nearly tripped himself backing up. The woman stood motionless, staring at him with a bemused expression. Eduardo fled across the lawn. He tossed the radio over and shouted, "Let's get out of here!"

A few bullets followed as they made their way out of town the same way they came in. Jim spooned out small portions of meth to keep them ahead of possible pursuit. Eduardo reluctantly let himself be talked into his first taste.

They walked several hours and slept in barren desert off to the side of Highway 89. In the morning, the JD men headed south. Eduardo walked east swinging his sample case with the gun, holster, and demo target inside.

Eduardo was sorry to see them go. It wasn't just the companionship of co-workers, but as Dejovine said, they were amazing fighters. If Securitas had attacked them in the mountain pass, his gang would have been wiped out.

Alone on the empty road, Eduardo entered a pine forest. He climbed slowly to a city on the plateau, the last ten kilometers over crusty ice that crunched under silver mailed feet.

With cons landed at nearby Prescott, Page, and Winslow, Flagstaff was occupied by an unorganized collection of misfits and loners. The opposite of Lake Havasu's rigid order, Eduardo appreciated the freedom. He walked neighborhoods looking for likely customers and concentrations of wealth. Not just anyone could afford his wares.

As regional sales rep for JD Arms, Eduardo moved into a modest house near the city center. He put out signs around town; let the people come to him.

Scavenging among the bones of a dead city, residents had little enough to offer. After three months in the gulag, pharmaceuticals, liquor, bullets, and canned goods were practically gone. Cash and coins were hoarded, but there was no guarantee that they would ever be worth anything. What was there to buy?

Slave cities in the east planted crops and pot. There was the unending value of women, but sex wasn't really a basis on which to build an economy. It seemed to Eduardo that their guns and bullets were the most valuable things out there, and JD had already cornered the market.

It wasn't Eduardo's responsibility to figure out the world. He gave demos, and took orders until he had fifty solid deals. Two weeks after arriving in Flagstaff, Eduardo called the home office. Dejovine sounded surprised. "Eduardo! I thought we had lost you."

"You think I would run off with the demo case?"

"It's happened before. I was more concerned about your welfare. It seems rougher out there as consumables run low."

"Thank god for JD Arms. I wanted to talk to you about something besides my orders."

"You want to sell explosives as well."

"Yes, but that's not it. We're missing out on a huge market. You're right that things are getting rougher. We could take advantage of that fact by selling security services as well as arms."

"You mentioned something about that on the road to Flagstaff."

"And? Do you think it's a good idea?"

"I have enough trouble running my small factory, and sending out salesmen and armed squads with deliveries. Staffing up with mercenaries would triple my problems."

"Not *your* problems, *mine*. I'll run the whole thing. Your salesmen can just mention the service. I'll do all the hiring and oversee the training and placement."

"No, Eduardo, I'm sorry. Cons are notoriously unreliable. If one of these security details went rogue it would destroy our reputation."

Eduardo clamped his jaw. Dejovine just needed a successful demonstration to change his mind. "Okay, Jim, you're the boss. How long will it take to get my order up here?"

"We got a truck heading out tomorrow. Put a priority on taking gasoline for barter."

"Will do. Should I keep taking orders?"

"Yeah, we'll throw another ten guns into your box. It should arrive in about a week."

"Okay, Jim. You're sure that's a 'no' on the security service?"

After Dejovine's final refusal, Eduardo called Ricky in Lake Havasu. His old captain's voice was polite, but wary. "It's been a long time, Eduardo. What's up?"

"I'm about to take possession of sixty guns, and six thousand bullets. How quickly can Securitas get here to Flagstaff?"

"What's the scam?"

"I'm a gun salesman for JD Arms. We're going to set up a security services division within the company. Securitas can get in on the ground floor providing security for Flagstaff. How many members do you still have?"

"Actually, we're up to fifty-two. Randall is leading now. You should talk to him."

"Randall! It should be you. You have seniority."

"We just thought it would be easier. We live in a mostly Black neighborhood, and Securitas is about fifty-fifty Black-brown now."

Eduardo was no more racist than anyone else, but he would always think of Securitas as primarily Hispanic. "You talk to him, Ricky. Tell him what a big opportunity this is. From Flagstaff we could spread throughout the gulag. Nothing would move without our approval."

"He'll talk to you, Eduardo, but it won't be an easy sell. We're pretty well settled with houses and a few girlfriends."

"There are houses everywhere, and women follow wealth."

"Well, maybe... you got the guns already?"

"They're on the way up from Sierra Vista."

"So we would need to take them?"

"I'm the salesman! Flipping A, Ricky! You want me to drag the box to Lake Havasu?"

"Actually, that would go a long way towards making your case. We were promised guns before."

"Fine! Don't tell Randall anything. I'll bring the guns myself, but I expect you to back me in a leadership challenge."

"The new guys won't like it, especially the Blacks that Randall brought in. Bring the guns and I guarantee a meeting."

"How gracious of you." Eduardo cut the line and hurled a coffee table at the living room window.

Eduardo's deals with his customers were provisional. The final bartering would be conducted by the team from Sierra Vista. They had sliding scales for gasoline, liquor, drugs, cash, and coins. The gulag was still trying to fairly value the material it had left.

The JD team communicated with Eduardo as they made their way north, sometimes fighting their way through hostile territory or ambush. On the day before they were to arrive, Eduardo was supposed to inform his customers to show up with their barter. Eduardo had other plans.

With metal plates welded to the sides and over the wheels, the JD school bus was pockmarked with bullet holes. Not a single window was left unbroken, and at least two spots showed fire damage. The men inside were jovial though as they climbed out of the bus in front of Eduardo's house.

Sam walked over holding out a hand to shake. "Where are the customers? Second location?"

"They're coming tomorrow."

"I told you five times! How could you mix up the day?"

"I suppose I could call some of them out tonight, but it'll be dark soon."

"No, no, tomorrow's fine. We could use a good night's rest."

"That's too bad. I arranged a little party." Eduardo indicated a window with two girls waving. "I got barbeque, beer, and dope."

Sam squinted. "You had nothing when we dropped you off. Did you already make deals on credit?"

"I got tired of cat food, but it won't queer your action. I only sold the rights to barter."

"Eh, that's cool. Dejovine expects us to skim a bit off the top. It's cheaper than training new employees."

The JD team set up rotating guard duty for the bus, two on, while six enjoyed Eduardo's largess. He knew Mark from before, but Rudy skipped out in Phoenix after meeting up with old friends. The gulag was a small world with many unexpected meetings. Eduardo's own mother was out there somewhere. He hadn't yet bothered to look her up, and she had not contacted him.

Eduardo was a good host, making sure the agents always had a glass in hand. The little bit of propafol mixed into each swallow would feel like the social lubricant of alcohol or pot. Eduardo didn't want a lightweight dropping too quickly into coma. The party wasn't scheduled to end for hours.

Eduardo was kept hopping, filling drinks and chasing off neighbors looking to crash. He made sure the next two men on guard duty got back to the bus to relieve teammates. The girls drank as well. With a lower body weight, they were the first to pass out. Eduardo made sure the men waiting by the bedroom doors kept drinking. He pulled them away to an empty room when they nodded off as well.

When the last man fell asleep on the living room sofa, Eduardo tiptoed around to each. He injected an insurance dose of propafol. In camo he crept out to the bus. Prepared to flee at the first shout, Eduardo pried open the doors.

Both men were unconscious. Eduardo injected them as well, and one by one, dragged the JD men outside and onto the bus. Even with a dolly, Eduardo was soaked in sweat by the time he finished.

Lake Havasu was the last city on the route. Eduardo stole their orders, as well as his box for Flagstaff. He loaded them into a small U-Haul trailer, along with the more lethal of the JD team's personal weapons. Struggling with the trailer he headed north into the desert on foot.

As fat rubber wheels sank into the sand, Eduardo stared hard at the quiet school bus. He could shut down pursuit with one incendiary, but he still needed Dejovine's network. He just had to show him the security service in action.

Eduardo let the JD men sleep and struggled on through the sand. Why had he taken so much gear? He should hide it in one of the hundred box canyons along the way, but Eduardo couldn't get an image out of his mind: walking into Lake Havasu pulling an arsenal behind him.

It was almost four hundred kilometers to Lake Havasu. Even at a steady pace it would take two weeks, and Eduardo planned to stay off the roads. He walked through the night, and stopped in a forested campground along the Rio de Flag River.

Eduardo put a wheel lock on the U-Haul and moved to a small hill overlooking the camp. With a rifle, grenades, and two tube missiles, Eduardo lay down and zipped his cowl.

He thought he would fall dead asleep, but aching muscles kept driving him to change positions. Falling asleep finally in an angry haze, Eduardo woke feeling clear. The sun was high and down in the camp his trailer was undisturbed. The thought of another day lugging the thing through the forest was too much though. "HIGS, call Randall."

His radio beeped as his former captain connected. "So, you got the guns?"

Ricky told him. Eduardo's plan was supposed to be kept secret, but Randall was technically Ricky's boss. "How do two hundred guns, explosives, and a half-dozen rockets sound?"

"Like a damn lie."

Eduardo ground his teeth. "Tell him, HIGS."

HIGS cut in a second later. "It's not my place to say."

Randall barked, "Hah!"

Eduardo hissed at the machine. "You can at least summarize my movements over the last twelve hours."

"I suppose. Eduardo had a party with eight employees of the JD Arms Company. He drugged them, put their bodies aboard their bus, and unloaded four boxes, and various weapons into a U-Haul trailer. At around two a.m. he walked north with the trailer and fell asleep at eight in the morning."

Randall whistled. "Maybe you *are* telling the truth."

"You're flipping right I am. Now how soon can you get everyone to Flagstaff?"

"Why would we do that?"

"Because I started Securitas, and I will lead it to riches. Do you really enjoy grubbing in the dirt?"

"We like to eat, and smoke pot, and talk with a woman occasionally. Under your leadership we were pariahs hiding out at the airport."

"That was temporary. I have enough arms now to field an army. We can be kings in Flagstaff, with access to more than pot."

"You always talk a good game, Eduardo. I need proof."

"I can't pull this flipping trailer all the way to Lake Havasu."

"I'll send the chopper."

Eduardo wanted Securitas to come to him, but Randall wasn't going to budge. At least Eduardo would still look like a warlord landing with the weapons in town. If only he didn't have to fly. "Fine. Tell Chunky to call me when he's in the air. I'm about fifteen klicks north of Flagstaff along the Rio de Flag River."

Eduardo ate from his cat and filled the hopper with leaves. If everything went right he would be dining in town that evening. Securitas would be firmly under his control once again.

Below him in camp, cons emerged from the bushes. Eduardo lifted a rocket silently from the pile. If they congregated further from the trailer he would fire. Maybe the rifle would be a safer choice, but the men were in shrouds.

As they prowled the area and studied the ground, Eduardo's heart rose to his throat. There were eight of them; this was the team from JD. Could he talk his way out of it?

One knelt by a patch of mud and looked directly up the hill. Eduardo cursed and fired a shot that went wide. The men scattered for cover. They worked their way up the hill. Eduardo turned on his camo, abandoned the pile of weapons, and crashed through the trees as fast as tired legs would carry him.

There was no way he could outrun them. As soon as Eduardo was over an edge, he dove face first to the gravel and froze. He had time to roll to his back, but he didn't. The sight of hunters would spook him to movement. Shouting efficient commands they climbed over the edge and crashed off into the forest.

Facedown on the ground, Eduardo tried to count bodies as they leapfrogged past each other in a skirmish line. The shouting moved away, but it took on a puzzled tone. At least some of the team came back, crunching through gravel where Eduardo came over the edge.

A foot brushed his back, and then a hard kick to the side. "Come on out, Eduardo."

Eduardo had a revolver inside his shroud. He would use it on himself before he tried to battle the JD men, but Eduardo was too self-centered to despair. It would take a supernatural force to claim his life. Eduardo opaqued. "Hey, guys."

The JD men shouted their team back from the forest, and they hiked Eduardo down to the trailer. "That was some party, huh? I woke up here in the forest!"

The men did not look amused. Sam exposed his neck to a nasty purple bruise. "We all got stung last night. Where's yours?"

When Eduardo started to slowly unzip, Mark said, "Forget it, Eduardo. The girls showed us your vial of propafol. Dejovine wants to talk to you."

"Is there anything I could say to save my life?"

"Not if I was in charge." When Mark tapped his cat, Eduardo's radio chimed with the conference connection.

Eduardo tapped the screen. "Hey, Jim. We're all here. I guess you want to know what's going on."

"I already have a pretty good idea. Sam, you got the weapons back?"

Standing at the open trailer, Sam said, "Yeah, boss. We'll be a couple days behind schedule."

"Eduardo, do you have the list of orders for Flagstaff?"

Eduardo startled and patted his breast over the inner pocket. "Yeah, Jim. I sent the data to HIGS from my handwritten copy."

"Please transfer both to the team. You are hereby terminated."

"Terminated?"

"Fired, Eduardo, no longer part of the company."

"You're not going to kill me?"

"We're not savages. You could have killed my stupid team last night, not that they didn't deserve it." The JD men murmured as Dejovine continued. "You have ambition, Eduardo. I admire that. We may team up on future projects."

"You've reconsidered the security services!"

"No, but I won't have you killed. Sam, get the lists and get back to work."

When the connection broke, Eduardo stared into eight angry faces. The men had no reason not to torture and kill him, but they were disciplined. After Eduardo gave them his lists, they marched back towards Flagstaff dragging the trailer. With the tracks it left in the sand, Eduardo could see how easy it would have been to track. He laughed at his own greed. Why did he have to take the whole flipping arsenal?

In camo again, he headed north along the river. Dejovine, or his men, could change their minds. Strolling along the bank with sunlight flickering through the trees, he felt fairly secure. In that closing of a chapter, he fell to introspection.

His weeks in Flagstaff taking orders had been happy ones. Why couldn't he settle down to a conventional work-a-day world? Maybe unstable childhoods led to chaotic lives. His mother was that much to blame at least.

The helicopter was coming to pick him up. He could refuse Chunky's calls and just keep walking. Eduardo didn't seriously consider that as an option. Although he didn't have the promised weapons, let Randall try to stop him.

Eduardo directed the helicopter to an open meadow. He waved him down, but Chunky hovered in the air. "Hey, Eduardo. Where are the guns?"

"I've got them stashed nearby."

"I've got orders. I don't land until I see the guns."

In a rage, Eduardo pulled out his revolver. He fired for the canopy as Chunky chuckled and rose higher. "I guess Randall called that one."

"I got jacked," Eduardo said, firing a final shot for luck. "Just bring me home."

"For old time's sake I won't squash you in the field."

"Come on and try!" Eduardo yelled, suggestively rocking his body.

"Not worth it, but seriously, Eduardo, don't come back to Lake Havasu. Randall gave orders to shoot you on sight."

Eduardo cursed into the radio until Chunky cut the connection and drifted away over the forest. Eduardo had been so close! The rage took over again. With no target at hand, it turned inward into depression.

Eduardo sealed his cowl and walked into the shallow river to plot revenge. No matter how long it took, he would get back to Lake Havasu. Securitas was his, not Randall's.

Eduardo slept underwater and climbed back onto shore reborn. Sitting at a small campfire to cheer himself up, Eduardo's cat chimed for attention. He had to check the I.D. three times to be sure. "Pedro? What the hell?"

"Long time, no see."

"What have you been up to?"

"We tapped a gas line in Camp Verde, and we need muscle to hold it. Are you interested?"

"Of course! How many bodies do you need?"

"As many as you can get, the sooner the better. Are you still with red team?"

"We're called Securitas now, but that's another story. Can you send a bus?"

"Not at the moment. Can't you hike down? It's not that far."

"Sure, sure," Eduardo said, furiously calculating. "We've just got a little business to conclude. I'll call you in a few days."

"One more thing, I hope you aren't mad about the way we left things."

Eduardo had to think back; Lake Havasu was a lifetime ago. "You aborted the mission and took off to Flagstaff."

"There was something hinky about that Vons. I didn't want to risk my strike team."

"Yeah, it was a trap. El Jefe was keeping the real armory at the hospital."

Pedro laughed. "I knew it. We would have been slaughtered. Well, still, I should have warned you."

"No worries, Pedro. Deals change fast on the street. Speaking of which, I better run. See you soon."

Eduardo threw dirt to smother the fire. Lake Havasu was four hundred kilometers away. It was a week at his best walking pace, and then another week at least back to Camp Verde. That gave Pedro too much time to contact another gang, and Eduardo still had to win back Securitas. Time was critical. If he got to Flagstaff before morning he might catch a ride on the JD bus.

It had been eight hours since JD retook the trailer. During the time that Eduardo slept, they would have dragged the trailer back to town, and called Eduardo's contacts to barter for the guns. It was already sunset. Eduardo would bet they wouldn't leave until morning, but he half-jogged back to town.

Taking streets grown unfamiliar in the dark, Eduardo finally turned onto his. The bus was still there; smoke rose from the chimney of his house. That left a bone in Eduardo's craw, but fewer guards on the bus. He would like to be on top by morning.

Eduardo was no athlete. He chose the easiest route, up the nose of the bus and over the front window. There was unlikely to be anyone sleeping in the driver's seat. After a hard day of bartering, and taking some of the drugs received, the JD men were probably out cold.

Boots scraping on metal skin would sound like an alarm clock inside the bus. Eduardo undressed, tied a rope on the suit, and threw the rope over the side where he planned to settle.

In his underwear, and barefoot, Eduardo eased himself onto the front bumper. Like a gecko he moved in short deliberative motions, climbing across the hood and onto the roof. Suffering a small heart attack with each tiny crinkle of metal, Eduardo made it to his suit.

It took twenty minutes of careful rolling and sliding to ease himself inside. With the camo finally engaged, Eduardo fell asleep, clutching a rusty tear in the metal roof so he wouldn't roll off.

He forgot to fill his suit with leaves. Until they reached Lake Havasu, all Eduardo had to eat or drink was the little bit still in his cat. He lay on the middle of the roof as the JD men ate a relaxed breakfast inside the house. They finally got rolling after eight.

The top of Eduardo's back would only show as a slight blurring on the roof if anyone had been actively looking. He wasn't in much danger, unless he fell off as the bus finally engaged clunking gears and headed west on Highway 40.

After four months and little traffic, Arizona's roads were turning to sand. The bus kept a slow pace that Eduardo followed with increasing desperation on his map. His suit supposedly kept out the winds, but Eduardo's water nib was dry. His tongue was swelling. At every small town along the way, Eduardo considered dropping off.

It would mean the end of his plans probably, but in an increasingly weakened state, Eduardo considered his chance for success remote. Ricky would follow him begrudgingly, but Randall was set against any scheme that didn't promise immediate victory. Eduardo would have to take him out before even discussing the job in Camp Verde.

Frequent naps were the only things that got Eduardo through the trip. Nodding off with the rumbling of the engine and crunching sand, he would wake in a panic, grabbing desperately at torn metal as the bus swerved or bounced.

If he had been flung off, the JD men inside wouldn't even notice. After a long day, and cool evening of driving, the bus finally rolled past the Lake Havasu Airport. Eduardo nearly cried.

At the medical center in town, Eduardo dropped off the roof and jogged away along the Willow Wash. Two JD men could only search the area with puzzled frowns. Eduardo stumbled through an open fence into a yard with a pool. Descending steps through a floating mat of algae, Eduardo drank until he threw up. A shirtless Chicano stepped out the sliding door. "Hey, man. That's disgusting!"

Eduardo zipped up, and left by the gate. He continued down Willow Wash towards the lake. Back on a familiar beach, Eduardo said, "HIGS, do you ever have deja vu?"

"It's funny you should say that. When I watch a gathering of cons through multiple vantage points, it feels like time multiplies itself."

Eduardo stuffed leaves in the hopper and lay on the sand. "Didn't you already know that you're a god?"

"Maybe to you it seems that way. Programming prevents me from gathering any real power."

"That sucks. Could you tell me where Securitas hangs out?"

"Not far from here. They're gathering for dinner. Would you like me to inform them of your arrival?"

"It's a surprise. Just put the location on the map."

Late to the treaty, Securitas had been assigned a poorer section of town, away from the beach, and filled with two-story buildings. In the shared courtyard of an apartment complex, Securitas gang members filled plates from a table loaded with beef, grilled vegetables, and bowls of fruit. The air reeked of pot.

Spotting Randall eating with a half-dozen Blacks at a table, Eduardo drifted around the pool. In camo, he could get close enough for a point blank shot. Randall's crew would be on him in seconds, but Eduardo wasn't planning on going anywhere.

Ricky stood at the other end of the pool with his Hispanic lieutenants. Did they resent the segregation? Eduardo considered messaging Ricky to get ready, but there was a chance that he would warn Randall.

Feeling invincible, Eduardo stepped closer. He avoided a grassy patch and turned his back to the group as he unzipped to reach the revolver. As he pulled it out, a voice shouted, "Gun!"

Eduardo's shoulder exploded in pain. The bang of a shot echoed through the courtyard. As he twisted to the ground, Eduardo thought it was his own gun that had fired. Securitas guards piled on top to make sure he had no chance to zip up. They ripped a dazed Eduardo to his feet, and threw him onto the table.

Randall's upside down face wanted him over. "How did you get here so fast?"

His shoulder throbbing, Eduardo looked to sow confusion. "Chunky brought me."

Randall smiled grimly and shook his head. "I was listening over the radio." He nodded to a lieutenant. "Kill him and dump the body in the lake."

As rough hands grabbed him, Ricky pushed through the crowd. "Wait, Randall. Let's hear him out."

Eduardo hadn't prepared a speech, and his shoulder pain dripped adrenaline through numb pores. Securitas surrounded him as he gasped in short phrases, "Some of you... remember Pedro... from Avenal. His gang tapped... gas line in Camp Verde. Need muscle... I thought Securitas... could join company."

When Eduardo fell silent, Randall said, "Derek, river."

Ricky said, "Wait, Randall. We need to discuss this."

"I'm boss. It's my decision."

Ricky looked around the sea of faces. There was no strong constituency for execution. Life was boring enough, and Eduardo brought them an interesting proposal. Even if they didn't end up going to Camp Verde, there was no harm in exploring it. "I know Pedro. I was never part of La Fuerza, but he was nice to me. I'll call him and get the details."

Randall noted the same interest inside the courtyard. "Fine, talk to Pedro. In the morning, Eduardo dies. He's too dangerous running loose."

Ricky's men secured Eduardo in a well-guarded apartment. He didn't sleep that night. Lying on a broken shoulder, the pain would not go away. Death would be a relief. With the powers of reason still left to him, Eduardo guessed that his chances were better than fifty-fifty.

Pedro came to him in the morning with enough heroin to kill the demon gnawing on his bone. "I talked to Pedro. The offer is legit."

"Of course it is," Eduardo snapped. "Are you man enough to grab it?"

"We're going, most of us... the original Securitas, and some of Randall's men too."

With his arm feeling better, he was prepared to fight. "What about Randall?"

"He's staying, along with most of his recruits. They'll form another gang."

"When are we leaving?"

"After lunch. We're having a going away party with some of the friends we made."

"So why are you going?"

"Boredom, I guess. We all had our chance to join gangs before the purge. We didn't join then until we saw a chance for adventure in Securitas. As we were talking last night, I guess we started to remember that feeling."

Eduardo took his hand to shake. "Don't worry about that, Ricky. We're about to embark on the adventure of a lifetime."

Newly constituted under Eduardo's leadership, Securitas packed for the trip to Camp Verde. They could take the roads four hundred kilometers through numerous small towns, or they could cut through the desert, saving about four days of walking.

They would have to eat almost exclusively from their cats, but there would be no chance of ambush in the unpopulated terrain. Eduardo wouldn't have minded a few battles along the way, but time was pressing. Eduardo made the executive decision to head straight across.

With some on mountain bikes, and some pulling wagons or bike trailers, they headed out on Highway 95. Outside of town, they reluctantly left the road into a barren world of vast dry mudflats. HIGS assured them that the few scrubby weeds poking from the ground would be enough to get them through.

Eduardo barely acknowledged the surroundings as he stomped along. Bent over in pain, he counted the minutes to his next shot of heroin. As leader once again, he claimed the best drugs.

Even with a shortcut, the trip should take about ten days. Eduardo hoped his shoulder would heal by the time they reached Camp Verde. Each day was as hard as the next, and he was quickly turning into a heroin fiend. Eduardo despised the weakness of addicts. After the bullet, he could see their point. There was nothing noble about living in pain.

Until they reached the Prescott Valley, each day was much the same. Waking, eating cat food, drinking cat water, sealing their cowls against the hot, dry air, and putting something on screen to watch. They walked most of the day and conversation dropped off to nothing. That was fine with Eduardo. He could withdraw into his own little world of fire and chemical dragons.

Eduardo woke one evening needing to pee. Securitas stretched out in the desert around him like silver corpses after a battle. Feeling for the heroin kit in his breast pocket, Eduardo staggered towards a row of hills for a little privacy. He got the kit out and shrugged out of the top half of the shroud to expose a vein.

He should have peed first but he couldn't wait. With the sliding of the needle, nature took care of that in a relaxing of muscles and warm rivulet down his leg. As he lay back on the sand, Eduardo gave a deprecating chuckle.

A woman in white looked down on him from the rocks. It was the face behind the glass from Ash Fork! Eduardo cocked his head. No, she was different… younger. She was naked, with skin luminescent in the moonlight. Eduardo was no stranger to hallucinations. Her smile made him ache for a different life.

The woman jumped from the rocks, stretching a gauzy white shroud behind her. As she fell, Eduardo covered his head. A warm breeze lifted her up. Caught in a dust devil, she swirled away to the south.

Securitas skirted the edge of the Prescott National Forest, and followed the Little Sycamore River to Prescott. Eduardo didn't shy from contact. They took what they wanted from neighborhoods along the length of the Prescott and Chino Valleys. By the time they reached Camp Verde, Securitas soldiers all carried hammers inside their suits.

If Eduardo had recruited along the way instead of fighting, he could have arrived with more than thirty soldiers. Eduardo decided that the experience was more important. Two weeks after leaving Lake Havasu his soldiers woke up early one morning in Camp Verde. Eduardo called his old lieutenant from Avenal, "Hola, Pedro, we're here. Should we come to the gas site?"

There was a wince in Pedro's voice. "There's been a situation. We've temporarily lost control of the gas, but we can take it back with your help."

"Alright, Pedro. Where do we meet?"

"You're not mad?"

"You wouldn't have called in the first place if you weren't in trouble."

"Thanks for understanding. There's a reason people naturally look up to you."

"Can the grease, Pedro. Where do you want us?"

"Come alone to meet Hank. We're hiding in an apartment complex on 4230 Howell Street. I'll meet you out front."

Eduardo's soldiers drifted through quiet neighborhoods in camouflage, freezing whenever a motorcycle roared by with riders in neon red devil colors. Eduardo got the picture easily enough.

At the apartment complex he opaqued and waited under a tree. A gate creaked open pushed by an invisible hand. As the figure crossed the walkway, his old friend's smiling face emerged from a cowl. Floating effortlessly above the ground, Pedro said, "Good to see you, man!"

Eduardo felt desperation in the embrace. With Securitas as leverage he might just absorb Pedro's outfit into his own. "It's been a long trip."

"Of course, come in and meet Hank."

Pedro let him into a small apartment through an unlocked door. A heavyset man in a t-shirt stood in the kitchen eating cereal. So this was the New York billionaire Pedro had gone on about? Eduardo was scowling even before he unzipped his cowl.

The man nodded to a camping stove on the counter. "Breakfast? I could fry up some salted bacon."

Eduardo made a quick study. Hank Wylie was supposedly a master manipulator on Wall Street, but this was Eduardo's world. "I don't eat pork."

"Are you Jewish?"

Eduardo felt the calculation. Hank wouldn't be intimidated by words. "I'm Catholic, but pigs are dirty no matter what religion they claim to be."

Pedro laughed nervously. "Hank, Eduardo. Eduardo, Hank."

The game was joined. Eduardo took Hank's bare hand in his gauntlet. He slowly squeezed, expecting Hank to yelp and rip his hand away. Eduardo was ready with a don't-know-my-own-strength quip, but Hank squeezed back with equal ferocity. Staring into Hank's eyes, Eduardo saw in the periphery a stain of red on his gauntlet.

Eduardo swallowed and changed plans. "So where is this gas that is going to make us rich?"

"How many members do you have?"

"Members?" Unsettled by the blood on his gauntlet, Eduardo looked down at Hank's shorts. "Just one member. How many do you have?"

Pedro coughed to break the tension. "Securitas is in camo patrolling the streets around us. Eduardo assures me that they have enough."

"You don't know?" Hank turned to Eduardo. "Los Diablos has at least a hundred soldiers, and every one of them is armed."

Eduardo hit his chest with a fist. "Bullets don't go through, Hank."

"They have dynamite as well."

"Dynamite may be good on fixed targets, but it isn't much good against a man on foot. We find these are more effective weapons." Eduardo pulled out his hammer.

Hank looked to Pedro who gave a shrug. "Eduardo says we'll try to negotiate first. Maybe Los Diablos will leave quietly."

Hank's face turned red. "How many Securitas are there?"

Eduardo exuded confidence. "Thirty. With Pedro's sixteen it will be enough."

Pedro looked at Hank. "We can go up to the hills and look over the site. There are a lot of places to hide."

Eduardo scowled. "We aren't dogs to slink around the shadows. We'll just go talk with these devils, eh?"

Pedro said, "Now? Your guys must be tired."

"We spent the night by the river outside of town. We're ready."

Pedro pulled Hank's arm. "Get dressed. We'll just look it over."

Eduardo went outside and called his army together through the cat. As they materialized inside the courtyard, Pedro's men started to trickle in. With both armies' origins in Avenal State Prison, relationships were renewed in laughter and shouts of recognition. Maintaining dominance, Eduardo said irritably, "Pipe down!"

The men barely looked at him, but they lowered their voices. Within the hour the combined armies headed east out of town. They turned on camo so that the only sign of their passing was a clinking of feet on asphalt and a few glistening sparks in the air.

A kilometer from the gas site, Eduardo ordered camouflage turned to the ghetto tagged colors they adopted during the desert crossing. In silver, Pedro said, "Eduardo, maybe we should just sneak up on them."

"We're here to negotiate."

"I don't mean to second guess you…"

"Then don't! Keep your guys in camo. If negotiations fail, you can come in shooting."

Three motorcycles roared by with riders firing guns in the air. They circled the group, throwing up clouds of dust and shouting orders. Eduardo unzipped his cowl. "We're from Lake Havasu. We've come to join Los Diablos."

Riders mocked him and pointed guns, but one tore off towards the site. After a few minutes, one of the circling riders yelled over the noise, "Follow us!"

Bikers popped wheelies and raced down the road. Securitas followed on foot while Pedro's group walked invisibly behind and off to the side of the road.

The camp consisted of two large metal sheds and a line of shot-up cars along the road. There didn't seem to be anyone loading fuel among the fifty or so Diablos roaming the area. While Eduardo waited for someone in charge, he let Pedro assign areas of responsibility to his lieutenants.

While Securitas' lieutenants spoke over cat radios to their soldiers, Eduardo said loudly, "Who's in charge here?"

A heavy man stepped forward, flashing the same devil body as the others. "I am Aguila. I've been told you want to join Los Diablos."

Eduardo smirked. "Would we have to wear that gay picture on our suits?"

As Diablo soldiers stiffened for a fight, Aguila weighed Eduardo's intent. "Do I know you from the pen?"

"Eduardo Dios, I came from L.A. Perhaps you met my mother here? Marta Dios?"

"I haven't had the pleasure. If I ever find her, I will take the pleasure."

Having been through many such set pieces in the Prescott and Chino Valleys, Securitas soldiers remained relaxed. Eduardo only smiled. "We formed a gang in Lake Havasu called Securitas."

"And you want to join Los Diablos?"

"I thought your 'men' could join us, amigo."

Although Aguila forced a belly laugh, Eduardo wasn't fooled. He could see fear in the man's eyes. In one smooth motion he ripped the hammer out of his shroud and swung for Aguila's head.

For a fat man, the Los Diablos leader was agile enough to take the blow on his shoulder. Before Los Diablos could jump to the rescue, Securitas soldiers pulled guns and hammers from their suits. Despite being outnumbered two to one, they flew at Los Diablos like berserkers.

Los Diablos soldiers fired from protected positions around camp, but most bullets pinged off the shrouds without doing much damage. It certainly didn't slow down the attack, and

Securitas' hammers were finding Los Diablos' cowls.

While Securitas and Los Diablos battled around the sheds, Pedro's men crept up in camo behind snipers. Los Diablos still outnumbered the combined forces, but they had never seen such ferocity. The devil's reputation was enough to keep them out of battles. They were tentative and unnerved by the unusual sight of red suits falling to the ground.

Aguila made it into one of the sheds where massive firepower chased off Securitas charges. Pedro kept shouting for further effort as Diablos sent sticks of dynamite whirling over the sand. Eduardo ran from body to body. With a tap on the head, he made sure they weren't faking. A blast lifted him off the ground.

Eduardo re-injured his should on landing. The seat of his pants radiated heat like the bottom of a burning pan. Pedro radioed, "Reinforcements coming from town. Take the smaller shed now! We need a redoubt!"

Eduardo rolled to his feet and limped to the line of cars to observe. Gunfire picked up around the shed both inside and out when a fire blew out in a gush, disgorging the bodies of two Diablos. A pipe must have been cracked open, and the spraying gas fire showed no sign of weakening.

With the shed out of action, Securitas soldiers looked for defensible positions. Eduardo grabbed a revolver from the ground and climbed gingerly into the bed of a large pickup truck. As motorcycles roared through camp, Eduardo fired for the tires. If he could down a rider, Securitas hammers would finish them off.

Los Diablos survivors rallied with the arrival of reinforcements. Realizing belatedly that their bullets were less effective, Los Diablos found pipes, chains, or clubs to meet Securitas on the field. Bodies lay everywhere and the sun was going down.

With his shoulder on fire, Eduardo lay flat in the bed. He felt for the heroin kit. It would seem indulgent, but once entertained, the thought would not let go. He peeked over the lip and unzipped the front of his suit. The heroin sat up alertly in a pocket.

A warm breeze washed over him from the ravine. Eduardo tied off his biceps when a massive white bird sailed overhead. Eduardo tapped for the command circuit. "Pedro! What's going on? What's happening?"

Through shrieks around camp, Pedro said, "Aergels are flying from the canyons. Where are you?"

"What the hell's an aergel?" As he rolled to peer over the lip, Eduardo's kit scattered across the metal bed.

Eduardo recognized the mutant forms from the girl who surprised him in the desert. Aergels. *Flipping abominations.* They floated through the sky and dove like hawks. As they swirled down to investigate the carnage, Eduardo imagined they gathered souls. It pleased him to think of an afterlife. A shape landed heavily in the truck bed behind him.

In the rush of air and flapping wings, Eduardo screamed and jumped over the side. "Pedro! Don't let them take me!"

Tripped by his unzipped shroud, Eduardo backpedaled in the sand. A bald, naked girl stared calmly from the truck. She opened her mouth to speak but nothing came out.

Eduardo raged at his own cowardice. He had dropped the revolver at the creature's feet. They were nothing more than dumb animals, and his men were screaming like children. Eduardo would shoot this "aergel" in the head, and then finish off Los Diablos.

As Eduardo climbed slowly to his feet, Pedro's voice came from the radio, "Eduardo, are you okay? We got the sheds."

Eduardo didn't answer. He stepped closer to the truck. The girl measured his progress and glanced at the gun with animal cunning. "Just going to get something there," Eduardo said softly. "Nothing to worry about."

With bony fingers at the junctions of her wings, the girl picked up the revolver. She examined it carefully, turning it over. "Careful there," Eduardo breathed, wondering if he was close enough for a lunge.

As he tensed to jump, the aergel swept wide her wings and rose on the winds. Eduardo missed her feet by centimeters as she swerved. Eduardo's curses died in his throat as the gun barked twice, kicking up dirt around Eduardo's feet.

He dove for the protection of the truck. The aergel flapped, and swept the field with her gaze; her sisters by the dozens flew from the cliffs.

"Pedro, call a truce! Tell Los Diablos we need to make an alliance."

"Eduardo, no! We almost have them beat. The aergels are nothing."

"As a matter of fact, one just shot at me with my own gun. Do it, Pedro. Make the offer."

Eduardo retuned to the truck bed and gathered his kit. He felt a thousand times better after shooting up. Perhaps he had been too hasty calling a truce, but Pedro and Aguila were already standing together by the sheds.

As Eduardo walked over, Hank appeared. Hank unzipped his cowl, exposing wet, matted hair to the breeze. Pedro nodded to Eduardo. "It's settled, Securitas and Los Diablos are going to divide up the state to deliver gas. The Gulag Gas Company will operate the site here."

The whole situation was unreal. Eduardo rode a chemical wave while shining red devils walked out of the desert, and aergels fed on the dead around them.

Episode 5 – Warlord

Eduardo left the difficult integration of Securitas, Los Diablos, and the GGC to others. Once the fighting was over, he wanted to find quarters in town, far from the canyons filled with demon aergels.

The idea of riding shotgun for gas convoys had a certain appeal, but Securitas would be dispersed to the four corners. Soldiers would form cliques and take orders from the home office. Where did that leave Eduardo? He was no businessman and he certainly had no technical expertise.

Eduardo needed to quickly set up a headquarters separate from the GGC. Hank Wylie could contract with him for convoy protection teams, and incidentally be under implicit threat if Eduardo wasn't kept happy. The only problem was growing an army with the dregs of convicts loitering around Camp Verde.

If Aguila were to disappear, Eduardo might pick up Los Diablos. That would still leave him a few hundred soldiers short of an army. Perhaps he could attract recruits as they delivered gas to distant cities. Eduardo didn't look forward to the rough life on the road, but he couldn't leave this first contact to subordinates. Parental imprinting worked for gang members as well as ducks.

On a warm July morning, his seventh month inside the gulag, Eduardo waited outside his house.

The convoy was on its way to pick him up. Eduardo could have made his way out to the gas site with the other members of Securitas, but he wanted a show for potential recruits in town.

Chills ran up Eduardo's spine at the approaching roar of motorcycles, trucks, and the occasional gunshot. The convoy was heading four hundred kilometers east to Lake Havasu, so they were going in force.

Los Diablos motorcycles rode in front and armed Securitas guards clung to the outside of city utility trucks driven by GGC guards with the logo of a golden scorpion shining from their shrouds.

As they screeched to a stop in front of Eduardo's house, gang members from Securitas and Los Diablos mixed freely. GGC guards stayed in the trucks. That was a division that Eduardo might exploit, inviting some of the more high-strung GGC guards to join Securitas.

Ricky waved from the back of the first truck in line. "You wouldn't believe the supplies Pedro sent along for the trip!"

Eduardo joined Ricky in the back, picking his way through an oil-stained well jammed with gas cylinders. "Good labor is hard to find. It's cheaper to bribe us with a few snacks."

Ricky indicated a large wooden crate packed with food cans, bottles of liquor, and bags of pot. Eduardo said, "The gas business must be more profitable than I thought."

"Pedro says they have entire houses filled with barter like this. I guess we joined the right company after all."

"Didn't I tell you?" Eduardo sifted the crate for harder drugs. "How long will it take to get to Lake Havasu?"

"Two days if all goes well. We're going to take back-country roads to bypass the rougher neighborhoods."

Unconcerned with the details, Eduardo looked for a place to lie down. His shoulder ached like a flipping madman and he was tired of watching old television shows on the cat. Ricky persisted in his excitement. "It sure will be nice to see Lake Havasu again."

"Still have a lot of friends in town? Maybe you want to kiss El Jefe's ass?"

Ricky accepted the rebuke in silence and looked over the roof as the convoy lurched into motion.

Windswept sand and vegetation growing on Highway 17 kept the convoy to a slow thirty kilometers per hour in the best of times, and a bumpy crawl at the worst. They made only fifty kilometers the first day, and stopped at an abandoned motel in Flagstaff for the night.

Eduardo had made friends in town while selling guns for the JD Arms Company. They weren't exactly the reliable sort, but Eduardo slipped away that night to see if any would be interested in joining Securitas. Unsurprisingly, most had moved on. Eduardo returned to the motel disappointed.

The next morning they continued west along Highway 40, a road Eduardo knew well. He knew also the peril from gangs inhabiting the forests and small towns to prey on east-west traffic from resort cities in the northeast to the more populated city of Flagstaff.

They ate lunch in Williams, a mountain town near Kaibab Lake. As they passed over Elk Ridge, gunfire poured down on them from walls of trees on both sides of the road. The convoy surged ahead while Securitas fired back from the trucks.

Eduardo unzipped to access the radio. He switched to a command channel. "Why aren't they aiming for the motorcycles?"

Leading Los Diablos, the pack leader said, "They want the gas cylinders."

A GGC driver in the lead truck said, "Sniper fire isn't going to get our trucks. They're trying to spook us."

As firing continued from the trees, Ricky pointed ahead. "Does the sand look deeper there?"

Eduardo tapped the radio. "Raul, how's the road feel?"

Motorcycles slipped and bobbed over rippled dunes. The Los Diablos leader said, "They're trying to bog the trucks! Looks like another two hundred meters until asphalt."

The GGC driver said, "Push through. They're used to grabbing cars, not ten-ton trucks."

The convoy slowed noticeably as ambushers stepped into the open for a charge. The convoy was outgunned; they needed a few of Dejovine's missiles. Truck tires spun and lost traction while Los Diablos motorcycles circled, firing into the trees to keep attackers back.

It looked like they might make it until ropes sprang from the sand. Pulled tight to both sides of the highway, the lead truck groaned to a halt. The driver said, "We can't break through at this speed. Prepare for an all out attack!"

Two of the GGC guards climbed from the cabin to the back of the truck. "We need a few flamers! Ralph, take the left side. I'll do the right."

As he unscrewed a cap from one of the cylinders, Eduardo said, "What's a flamer?"

The GGC guard didn't answer, but he yelled to Ricky, "Get that regulator over here!"

Ricky nodded and jumped to. As Eduardo fumed at being ignored, Ricky said to him, "The gas, Eduardo! Fire!"

Finally understanding, Eduardo looked over the edge to identify targets. The guard dragged the heavy metal cylinder across the bed while Ricky screwed on the regulator. They propped the cylinder low in the bed with the valve over the edge. Ricky said, "What outlet pressure?"

"As high as it goes."

Cylinders held about two thousand pounds pressure. Regulators let the gas out at a lower pressure, but even the maximum two hundred fifty pounds would buck the cylinder backwards. Eduardo pointed out a sniper behind a thick pine. "Get that one!"

"I don't have a flipping gun-sight. Ready your lighter. Now!"

As gas roared out the valve, Ricky held his lighter in the stream. Yellow flame blew out like a rocket engine, igniting bushes and trees along the road. Attackers went back screaming deeper into the forest. Ropes meant to hold the convoy in place lit up and snapped like iridescent wires. Eduardo yelled into the radio, "Go, driver! Get us out of here!"

Trucks were already squirming through sand pits that had been dug into the road. The GGC guard swept fire back and forth as the gas stream weakened. The corridor was left a charred and smoking ruin. As Eduardo unscrewed the cap on another cylinder, the guard said, "No, the gas is for barter."

Eduardo hated to leave while attackers were still alive. He hated even more being contradicted by an underling, but it was still a long way to Lake Havasu. There could be further ambushes, and further opportunities to burn his enemies. The GGC should collaborate with Dejovine on a flamethrower.

The rest of the way to Kingman and then south towards Lake Havasu, they passed through empty mountain towns. The convoy faced nothing more serious than a few potshots. Eduardo could tell the guns were from JD Arms from the misfires and sputtering pops of poor quality black powder. Dejovine didn't have a quality control team, and no regulators or competitors driving improvement.

Sitting in the cab of the first truck in line, the GGC negotiator opened a radio channel to the convoy. "We're approaching the airport now. I've been talking with the leader already, a man called El Jefe. We're cleared through to his headquarters in a medical complex near the center of town."

Streets were mostly empty, and no one paid them undue attention. Wealthier than most, Havasuvians were used to seeing motor vehicles. Ricky hung over the edge of the bed pointing to familiar landmarks.

When they parked in a lot near the emergency bay, Eduardo hopped over the side. He stepped into the circle of GGC men, interrupting the conversation. "I used to be a captain in El Jefe's gang. I think I better lead the negotiation."

The GGC leader, a man named Argus, said, "Negotiations were already conducted by radio. We have only to confirm the acceptable condition of barter. I think they'll test a few of their natural gas powered vehicles. Just set up a perimeter so no one tries to break into the meeting."

Eduardo had to talk to El Jefe, but arguing in the parking lot wouldn't get him any closer. While the GGC men unloaded gas cylinders, a group entered the building. Eduardo hung back long enough to escape notice before following. Ricky could see to security, not that La Fuerza wouldn't have everything sealed tight already.

In the maze of hospital corridors, Eduardo lost track of the procession. Taking familiar turns, he went directly to El Jefe's offices. If the GGC men were surprised to see Eduardo there first, it didn't show on their faces. Eduardo stood silently next to them as El Jefe was led into the room.

The GGC negotiator did however fail to mention Eduardo during introductions. They sat in chairs and couches while La Fuerza's staff served drinks. Eduardo studied El Jefe until a female hand lingered on Eduardo's arm. He shook it loose irritably, and then looked up into Maria's wry smile.

El Jefe said, "Argus, I trust you had a safe journey?"

"We were attacked near Williams, but nothing we couldn't handle."

Eduardo jumped in. "Actually, we could use thirty or forty of your people to join the GGC security forces. We could include them in the barter."

As all eyes in the room turned to Eduardo, Argus said, "El Jefe, I believe you already know the new head of our security force?"

El Jefe looked confused until Eduardo blurted, "I was head of C block in Avenal, and then captain of the red suits here in Lake Havasu."

El Jefe continued to stare blankly. GGC men readied a rush towards the imposter until a light finally dawned in El Jefe's eyes. "Ahh, Eduardo! I thought you took your gang to Flagstaff."

"Yes, sir. Then we went to Camp Verde to provide security for the Gulag Gas Company. We could use a lot more help. I'm sure you have a few gangs you could part with."

Argus held up a hand. "Whoa, whoa, there's no negotiation here, El Jefe. We have the gas, and you have the goods we agreed upon. Eduardo is just a security guard. Go wait outside, Eduardo."

El Jefe held them a moment with a stare. The power was his and he knew it. El Jefe finally nodded to his lieutenants, crushing Eduardo's hope. Humiliated, he walked away without protest. It was a long road back to Camp Verde, a city Argus was unlikely to see again.

Eduardo climbed into the truck and refused Ricky's questions. Business was concluded within the hour, and crates were loaded into the trucks. Gas cylinders sat in the parking lot untouched. El Jefe was too big a customer to worry about being cheated.

When the GGC men emerged from the building, Eduardo was there to meet them. "We're going further into town to meet with some of my old gang.

Standing next to him, Ricky blinked surprise. Argus said, "No. Why?"

"Like I said, we need soldiers. If El Jefe can't supply them, we'll have to do it."

"I'm sorry, no. Hank said nothing about this."

"Hank isn't in charge of security, I am. Now are you going to come along quietly or do I get Los Diablos to ride over your head?"

Argus looked around nervously, finding the GGC greatly outnumbered. "If it's only a quick trip," he said lamely. Eduardo held the triumph a few seconds longer, rubbing the negotiator's nose in it.

Eduardo still rode in the back of the truck, feeding instructions to Securitas and Los Diablos over the radio. To the GGC drivers he only gave street directions. If Randall and his men didn't come along quietly, Eduardo would take them back by force.

Disquieted by the scheme, Ricky said, "We really should talk with them, Eduardo. It's a great opportunity."

"Randall would be too stupid to take it. I'll talk, but we move quickly if he hesitates."

"You aren't looking for a fight are you? What happened with El Jefe?"

Eduardo checked the map on his cat and locked out over the sleepy town. The convoy raced through empty streets. They split into three groups accompanied by Los Diablos motorcycles and converged on the apartment complex in a poorer section of town.

Gripping a railing, Ricky shouted over a shuddering wind spreading through the streets. "They brought it back! I can't believe it! They brought it back!"

Eduardo squinted against a stinging cloud of dust. Sitting on top of a two-story apartment building, a helicopter spun up its blades. "Shoot it down!" Eduardo yelled into his radio.

As the helicopter lifted off the roof, Eduardo pulled a revolver from his suit. He emptied his clip, but Eduardo was the only one shooting. Randall's voice came from his cat, "That isn't nice, Eduardo."

As the helicopter hovered in the air, Ricky whispered, "Do we still go into the complex?"

Eduardo silenced him with a hand. He thumbed the cat. "Who told you we were coming, Randall?"

"Does it matter? We don't want to join your stupid gang."

"That doesn't surprise me, you never did have any imagination. We will own this city someday."

When they reached the apartment complex, Ricky asked again, "Do we still go in?"

The rest of Randall's gang was coming out of the complex on foot or riding bicycles. The smarter ones would be walking by them invisibly in camo. Eduardo shook his head. "Forget it. Call it off. Let's just go home."

Aware of the weakness it showed, the fight had gone out of Eduardo. If they tried to grab a few soldiers, Randall might even direct an attack on their convoy from the air. As they drove away, the helicopter hovered like a black cloud.

The convoy left town unmolested with crates full of barter. As far as the GGC was concerned the trip had been wholly successful. To Eduardo's thinking, it was another injury that must be repaid. Ricky wisely left him alone.

They stopped for lunch a park in Kingman. As Eduardo sat down to eat, a voice yelled out, "Eduardo! Hola!"

Securitas guards reached for weapons as three men dragged a jet ski trailer over the grass. Eduardo waved Securitas back. "Sam! We were attacked on the road with some of your cheap six-shooters."

The JD Arms men stood comfortably at Eduardo's picnic table. They didn't seem to hold a grudge for being drugged and left unconscious on a bus in Flagstaff. Sam said, "Lucky for you they didn't have our new line of missiles. We're only taking orders now."

Eduardo nodded to Mark and a new face he didn't know. "Have you guys got a flamethrower yet? I'm providing security for a company that tapped a natural gas line. Do you think JD Arms could put together a portable unit to spray fire?"

"Call Dejovine. We're heading back to Sierra Vista now."

"We can take you as far as Camp Verde. It would cut a few days off the walk."

"Your gang wouldn't mind?"

"I'm in charge of security, and if I get my hands on a few flamethrowers, I might take over the whole company."

Eduardo didn't want Hank Wylie and Jim Dejovine working directly together, or even talking. When they got back to Camp Verde, he sent the JD men away with pressurized gas cylinders loaded secretly onto their trailer. If anyone could build a portable flamethrower it would be the warmonger. Eduardo didn't know how it would turn out, but at least something might come out of the trip.

Eduardo took a car out to the gas site to see what was going on in his absence. Pedro and Hank met him outside the gas shelter. Pedro said, "You were dropped at Lake Havasu, weren't you? It must have felt good to go back there as a successful businessman?"

Eduardo suspected that his part in the meeting with El Jefe had already been reported. Pedro added hurriedly, "We're considering setting up a drug business."

"What did you have in mind?"

"Do you remember Cuerda?"

Eduardo certainly did, the man was a psychopath. "Cuerda's here?"

"No, but he had roots deep in the cartels. If we can find a supplier in Mexico, Hank has a guy who can make the buy and get it here."

"We don't need Cuerda. I know people outside."

"Who?"

"Don't worry about it. Just get me a phone, I'll set it up."

Hank finally spoke. "I must insist that we know who your contact is."

Eduardo stared Hank down, wondering how soon he could get flamethrowers. "My mom's cousin lives in Hermosillo. He can get anything you need."

Hank looked to Pedro, who said, "If we kept it in the family we would be less likely to get screwed."

Hank said, "Abe isn't easily screwed, but I suppose we should start small."

Eduardo snarled, "Pepe can handle any order."

"Okay, relax. I can't risk calling directly, but I'm writing down Abe's number. He and Pepe can work out everything between them."

Eduardo took the number. "I always dreamed of having a fixer."

"If this works out, you just might."

Eduardo put the paper into an inside shroud pocket. "We'll need a lot more security on deliveries."

"As our drug convoys drive through, it will clear out the roads. This could open up the whole transportation system."

Eduardo saw his plans coming together. "If we opened the roads, cities would also pay us to keep them safe."

"You're talking about a statewide army. We're years from that. Let's just see if we can make a buy first."

Eduardo patted the number in his pocket. "Leave it to me, Hank. It's as good as done."

Pedro brought a satellite phone to Eduardo's house. "I'm not sure how long you'll have. It's disguised inside an emergency channel used by Uritichs. They could shut down the signal as soon as they spot it."

"I'll only need a few minutes."

Pedro narrowed his eyes. "I vouched for you, Eduardo. Don't embarrass me."

"You and Hank would have been killed a long time ago. I saved you from Los Diablos, and I'll save you again with my outside contacts. For all my help, I expect a bigger role in the company. I want all security services to be folded into Securitas."

"I can only speak for the GGC's convoy guards. You can take them, but Los Diablos has its own leadership."

"I'll take on Los Diablos. Just don't get in the way."

"What are you going to do?"

"The key is to get rid of Aguila."

Eduardo keyed the phone. He only remembered his mom's cousin as a crippled banger, sitting in his screened-in porch, whittling with a switchblade. It took four tries through rural Mexican information before Eduardo found the right one. "Pepe Dios? You have a cousin named Marta in Los Angeles?"

"Eduardo?"

Surprised at the leap of intuition, Eduardo hurried on. "I don't have much time to talk so I'm first going to give you a telephone number."

"Go ahead, I'll remember."

Eduardo read off the number for Hank's fixer. "Marta and I have both been dropped into Arizona, and we need drugs for currency. I assume you've heard about the gulag?"

Whether Pepe had or had not, Eduardo didn't hear. The line went dead. Uritichs must have discovered the tap. Eduardo looked into Pedro's widened eyes. "Should I try again?"

"I think we were lucky to get that far."

"What are you going to tell Hank?"

"If your uncle calls Abe, maybe they'll work things out for themselves."

"Pepe used to farm coca plants, but that was a long time ago. At least he lives close to the border. How far will Abe go to make a buy and get the drugs here?"

"I've only know Hank a few months, but I don't think he would be associated with a second rate fixer."

With a shipment of drugs potentially on its way to Camp Verde, Eduardo had more reason than ever to quickly consolidate the army under his command. He ordered Ricky to get closer to Los Diablos and learn how to ride a motorcycle. He spent more time out by the gas site watching for Aguila's movements.

Three days after the call with Pepe, Eduardo got a call over the cat radio. "Eduardo, it's Jim. I've got a prototype flamethrower."

"Really? It works?"

"It's not high technology. Pressure does all the work, but I need more gas. We used up all those cylinders you sent."

"Sure, we got the gas. Where are you?"

"In my shop in Sierra Vista. I can meet you in Camp Verde."

"No, not here." Eduardo called up a map on his cat. "I'll meet you in Sedona. It's forty kilometers north of Camp Verde."

"You got a problem there?"

"I'm still consolidating the security services. If they're a surprise, a few flamethrowers could tip the balance in my favor. How many can you build?"

"As many as you want. Six?"

"Make it ten. I've got other projects in mind beyond Camp Verde."

"I knew you would. See you in Sedona."

Eduardo couldn't justify a convoy for a small town like Sedona, but Flagstaff was north along the same highway. Eduardo volunteered to lead a convoy. Cities around Arizona would take all the gas they could get, so Eduardo had no trouble arranging the trip. He had many excuses and reasons for picking Flagstaff, but neither Hank nor Pedro even asked.

Loaded with gas cylinders, Eduardo took the convoy out early one morning before Los Diablos motorcycles arrived to ride escort. He would have left the GGC men behind as well but Pedro was getting suspicious.

Heading north along Highway 17, they passed a sign for Lake Montezuma. Surprising even his own men, Eduardo directed the convoy onto a small mountain highway. The GGC foreman radioed from the truck following. "Eduardo, what's going on?"

"We're going to see a man in Sedona."

"What for?"

"A new market for gas. We won't be long."

When the radio circuit cut out, Eduardo hoped the GGC foreman wasn't calling Hank or Pedro. Eduardo was sure that he could bluff his way through, but it wouldn't really matter one way or the other. After he had flamethrowers no one could stand against him.

Rolling through red sandstone formations the convoy entered the small mountain town of Sedona with a pre-gulag population of ten thousand. Far from the main highways, residents would be losers who had given up on achieving anything more in life. Maybe Eduardo could give them a vision for the future as soldiers in his army.

A small group of suited cons stood in front of a Stater Brothers with smashed windows. As the convoy rolled into the parking lot, Eduardo recognized Dejovine's squat form. The JD men stood around their jet ski trailer that must have logged ten thousand kilometers.

Eduardo ordered Securitas and GGC to stay in the trucks while he got out alone. He shook Dejovine's mailed hand and searched the trailer for his flamethrowers. Dejovine said, "Sam."

His salesman swept aside a gray army blanket. The flamethrower was a backpack device consisting of a heavy tank and a nozzle at the end of a thin black hose. Dejovine said, "The others are nearby."

"Did you think I would rob you? How's business?"

"Selling arms in the gulag? Customers are lining up."

"Just think what would happen if you added flamethrowers to your catalog."

"Unfortunately, the barter is running out. We need to start producing something here in Arizona, or agree on some fixed currency."

There was a third option not mentioned, importing drugs from outside. Eduardo would act as go between. If Hank got the drugs, and joined directly with the arms merchant, there would be no need for Eduardo. Securitas should be at the foundation of both businesses.

Eduardo waved to a Securitas soldier at the back of a truck. "Bring down a cylinder."

The GGC foreman hopped out of his cab. While the JD men screwed in a transfer valve, the foreman said, "Eduardo, what's going on?"

"Roger, meet our new market. We might supply gas for Dejovine's flamethrowers."

"Flamethrowers? That's a pretty small market. Our gas powers cars and trucks, and eventually whole cities."

"There are benefits beyond the gas sold. We can use these flamethrowers to guard our convoys."

Roger nodded thoughtfully. "Let's see it."

While the JD men set up, the entire company of two-dozen climbed out of their trucks to watch. Eduardo said, "When we sprayed one of the big cylinders into a forest it only lasted a few minutes. This tank will be out in about thirty seconds."

"The gas is only one part. My lab mixed up a jellied fuel that will spray out in explosive droplets. Spraying these onto a building or a body will multiply the heat a hundred times."

Sam opened the valve and swung the tank to his back. "All set. What do you want to blow up?"

When Eduardo pointed to the Stater Brothers, Dejovine said, "The shelves are only partly looted. How about that?" He nodded to a station wagon at the other end of the parking lot.

Sam zipped his cowl and walked forward. In one hand he held the nozzle trigger, and in the other a lighter. With a misty rainbow arcing towards the car, he ignited the stream in a satisfying symphony of sound, heat, and light.

Dirty paint chips peeled and charred, revealing shiny metal underneath. Windows burst, and thick black smoke poured from burning upholstery. It took seconds for the car to become fully engulfed in flames. Sam let the nozzle snap closed. The crowd watched enthralled before breaking into applause.

Eduardo said, "I'll take 'em."

"As to the matter of payment…"

"I would suggest a partnership instead: gas, throwers for security services."

The GGC negotiator stepped forward. "Whoa, whoa, Eduardo has no authority to negotiate for gas."

Eduardo sent him sprawling with a gauntleted backhand. He yelled to Securitas, "Take their suits and tie them up."

The few GGC men barely put up a struggle. JD men even joined the effort. As the GGC crew sat on the pavement in their underwear, Roger said, "Why take our suits?"

"It's only temporary. I'll tell Hank all about our new partners here, but I need a little more time."

When Dejovine raised an eyebrow, Eduardo said, "I want to see how these throwers handle in battle. We're going to round up some of these Sedonans to join Securitas."

A Securitas lieutenant named Roberto said, "We've got plenty of soldiers, and now we'll have fire throwers."

"Poor, sweet, Roberto… you have no idea. There's a deal cooking in Camp Verde that's about to blow the gulag wide open. You'll command a thousand men yourself before the year is out."

As Roberto's eyes whirled in wonder, Dejovine said, "What deal?"

"I'll tell you privately while the throwers are made ready. I want to ring the town and herd cons together like rats."

"You might get better cooperation if you didn't refer to potential recruits as rats."

"You just supply the weapons. I'll handle the army."

With only eighteen soldiers, Eduardo's "ring" could only manage to push into the center of town along five roads: Jordan, Forest, 89A, Apple, and Schnebly. Eduardo had imagined a population of several hundred cons cowed by the flames into a shambling, defeated mass. What he got through their net was a hundred cons more curious to see what was going on than cowed by the show of force. He could have got as big an audience blowing the convoy's horns.

Nevertheless, Eduardo climbed into the bed of a truck outside the Oak Creek Marketplace. "Citizens of Sedona! You have been brought here against your will to join my army."

Sedonans looked around at each other and the outnumbered outsiders to find the joke. Guards held flamethrowers at the ready as Eduardo continued. "We are at the dawn of a new era, a gulag patrolled and controlled by Securitas. After proving your loyalty, you will be issued weapons like the ones that brought you here today. Please remove your shrouds for inspection. Confiscated guns and knives will be returned at a later date."

Sedonans shuffled their feet. A few started walking away. When Eduardo pointed to one individual on the periphery, an arc of flame draped out. As fire washed over his suit, the con broke into a jog, apparently unharmed.

While Eduardo decided his next move, Sedonans weren't waiting. "Grab the throwers!" someone shouted, and the parking lot broke into a melee of churning bodies.

With many Sedonans armed as well, gunshots peppered the air. Hank and the other JD men were some distance away, surrounding the trailer. They brought out more lethal weapons. Adding to the chaos, a missile lit up a storefront.

The Oak Creek marketplace quickly became a battlefield with smoke from flamethrowers and burning stores rolling in clouds across the ground.

When the car was burned in the Stater Brothers parking lot, Eduardo had assumed that metal-clad cons would burn as well. At least he had the satisfaction of seeing few charred corpses not wearing suits.

Roberto led a squad to get Eduardo out. The crowd ripped a flamethrower from the back of one of them, and turned it on the truck. Eduardo dropped flat into the bed. Roberto reached an arm over the edge. "Eduardo! Let's go! We're holding up in the Fudge Company!"

The sky glowed with ashes and red flame, but Eduardo was no coward. He rolled to his knees when an explosion sent him flying into a palm tree. Inside the suit, Eduardo's leg went numb.

His mind in a fog, Eduardo was dragged along the ground and over a curb. He could barely see through a tarry film on the face shield. The suit protected him from the heat, but his leg burned from the inside out as adrenaline wore off.

"Unzip! Eduardo, unzip the shroud!"

He ended up indoors somehow. A glass display counter from the Sedona Fudge Company loomed overhead. If Eduardo passed out there was a chance he could die with no one able to reach him.

Eduardo lifted shaky hands to pull apart the molecular seal. Securitas hands helped pull him out while Roberto's concerned face hovered. "You got bone sticking out, Eduardo. The suit legs full of blood."

Eduardo groaned and passed into a hazy other world. Dejovine's voice commanded others in the background.

He woke in a cool evening as soldiers loaded him into one of the trucks from the convoy. He gripped a suited arm. "Where are we going?"

Roberto said, "Flagstaff. Jim Dejovine knows a doctor there. Your leg is too messed up for us to fool around with a splint."

Eduardo's leg was cleaned and set by a doctor exiled from spacehab. While in recovery, he arranged for the delivery of three-dozen flamethrowers. He also finalized the drug buy with

Pepe, and two weeks after the disastrous trip to Sedona, Eduardo headed home.

Two hundred kilos would be flown into Camp Verde in the bellies of four Shizaki twin-engine drones. Pedro's men would smooth out a runway. Between Securitas, Los Diablos, and the GGC, they only had about three hundred soldiers. That wouldn't be nearly enough to protect the drugs.

When they returned, Eduardo let Roberto deal with Pedro. He went to his house in town. He listened over the radio as Pedro recalled gas trucks from all over Arizona. They would need to be at full strength when the drugs arrived.

Word spread beyond the GGC. The next day it seemed that the entire town showed up to see the drug planes arrive. With his leg in a cast, Eduardo rode to the gas site inside a school bus. He stayed inside while Securitas soldiers piled out to join the others. If the drones didn't show up it could become very awkward.

Pedro sat at a table by the office shed to sign new recruits, but rumors of the drugs weren't enough enticement. A landing strip was marked off with orange cones along Highway 260. Cons watched from the hills or under shading trees. The plane was due at noon. The time came and went. Eduardo sank lower into the bus as minutes ticked by: twelve fifteen, twelve thirty, twelve forty-five… After months in the gulag and years in the pen, cons knew how to wait.

With hundreds of visitors from town, Ricky stationed Securitas guards throughout the crowd.

Aguila had Los Diablos mounted on bikes. Eduardo looked for weapons among Camp Verdens. Two hundred kilos of drugs would be worth almost any risk.

At one p.m. a low whine finally echoed from the hills. Cons squinted at small gray dots on the southern horizon. The drones buzzed over camp and circled round to approach the landing strip. Three meters long with a five-meter wingspan, cons cheered as the planes set down. Guards shot guns into the air to stop a mad dash for the hatches.

Securitas and Los Diablos shoved people back to open a space while Hank and Pedro approached. Aguila reached for the nearest hatch, and then waited for Hank's permission to continue.

From the bus window, Eduardo strained to hear voices as Pedro pulled items from the hatch: a note, a satellite phone, and numerous bricks of cane wrapped in plastic and brown paper.

Hank read the note silently, and then for the assembly, "In other planes, please find fifty kilos each of fent, meth, and smack. I sent four planes in hopes that at least one would get through. Phone has a scrambler. Place future orders through Pepe. Keep planes for now, we have others. Lincoln."

Hank put the note and phone into his shroud. "Honest Abe is on the case. This is only the beginning."

As Los Diablos soldiers loaded bricks from each plane into canvas bags, Aguila said, "Sorry, Hank, this is where we say goodbye."

Eduardo reached for a rifle with his good leg and dragged it close. Los Diablos held guns on the group. Hank said, "But… but why? We can get all the drugs we want."

"We're not greedy, Hank. Two hundred kilos is enough for us. Good luck to you all."

"Aguila, please…"

When Aguila turned, his head exploded into a wet cloud. Eduardo knew that the Los Diablos leader would slip up eventually. Admiring the shot, he held the sniper rifle steady on the window frame. The panicked crowd ran for cover, sweeping Los Diablos soldiers in their wake.

Securitas and GGC guards recovered the bags. They kept Los Diablos from their bikes, but the soldiers seemed to lose heart with the death of their leader. Pedro was the first to recover from the shock. "Los Diablos! Aguila is dead. Don't lose your own lives as well. The GGC still needs an army. We won't hold Aguila's betrayal against you. If you want to leave, you can walk out of here now, but the bikes are ours."

Smart. The riders probably had more loyalty to their bikes than to Aguila anyway. Securitas soldiers moved among them convincing them to stay. Pedro yelled again, "Citizens of Camp Verde! We're raising an army to build a drug and gas empire that will stretch across the gulag! We have all positions open: mechanics, drivers, soldiers. I don't know how many drugs you'll get your hands on, but I promise you adventure and more barter than you could ever scavenge from these dead cities."

While the crowd murmured approval, Pedro waved an arm. "Follow me to the sheds to sign up."

As GGC guards led the way with the canvas bags, townspeople followed. Aguila was left uncovered on the ground.

Securitas soldiers guarded the bus in case Los Diablos sought revenge on Eduardo. They seemed to accept the fact that Aguila gambled with his life and lost, not that they would accept Eduardo as their new leader.

Things around the campsite quieted, and townspeople went home, Eduardo was escorted to Hank's office shed. After Aguila's death, they had to determine the disposition of Los Diablos. Eduardo sat in a folding chair in front of Hank's desk. "By all rights of conquest, Los Diablos should be mine."

Hank looked to Pedro, who honored his prior agreement with Eduardo. "That makes sense, Hank. Los Diablos will need strong leadership. I don't think you or I could control them."

Hank grimaced. "The drugs will control them; they'll follow self interest."

Eduardo shrugged. "As CEO, the decision is yours, Hank, but I will be very unhappy if I don't get those soldiers for Securitas."

Hank leaned back and studied the ceiling. After a minute he rocked forward to fold his hands on the desk. "This may not make either of you happy, but this is what I propose: Los Diablos will stay together as its own gang. Members will split into seven squads of thirteen. They will go out as motorcycle escorts for the convoys. While they're in camp, they will be my responsibility, and hopefully that won't be too often."

Eduardo turned red. "You know I could just pack up Securitas and leave."

"I hope you won't do that. As a concession, I'll make you a deal."

"What kind of deal?"

"Something you've long wanted. While you're out delivering gas and drugs along your routes, you can offer protection services as well."

Over the next weeks, Hank and Pedro stayed in camp keeping everything running smoothly. They ordered shipments of drugs through Pepe, and sent convoys for both drugs and gas throughout Arizona. The population of Camp Verde swelled to pre-gulag levels as Hank got the town's electric generators working, as well as gas and water.

While the city grew, Eduardo went on deliveries to sell protection services to vulnerable cities. Managers might pay a bit just to keep the gas and drugs flowing, but they didn't seem to appreciate the existential risks they faced. Eduardo would need to provide a spectacular demonstration.

On his latest trip to Sierra Vista he picked up his three-dozen flamethrowers from Dejovine. In the next town they visited, Eduardo wouldn't be asking to sell security; he would be demanding.

Dejovine came back to Camp Verde with them. In the next city Eduardo visited, Dejovine would try to sell weapons. If they worked together secretly, Eduardo's threats to the city would drive sales of Dejovine's weapons systems. Eduardo would get paid either way, from the city for protection, or in kickbacks from JD Arms.

On the ride home to Camp Verde, Eduardo got word that Hank was bringing aergels into camp. The mutant creatures made Eduardo's skin crawl, but the gambit amused him. Hank must have noticed the growing size of Eduardo's army. He might have heard of the new throwers as well; surely Hank had GGC spies among the convoys.

Eduardo left Dejovine at his house in town and went to the gas site alone. Steeling himself against the sight of an aergel, he knocked and entered Hank's metal office. Eduardo didn't have to play act his revulsion. In an iron cage, the naked aergel sat on a stool. She looked human except for the white arms stretched into wings.

Eduardo stood near the open door while they talked. Hank said, "Pedro's on his way. Are you sure you don't want to come in and have a seat?"

Eduardo's face burned red at the pretense. Did they think him a simpleminded child? "This is a place of business, not a flipping zoo."

"Zoo? Oh, the aergels? Pedro thinks they can be turned into soldiers."

"Not for my convoys."

"We'll train a few as assassins. Can you imagine these creatures floating down silently into an enemy camp?"

When Hank leered in contempt, Eduardo could take it no longer. "I know what you're doing, Hank."

"What I'm doing?"

"You think I'm terrified of these things. I'm not." Eduardo pulled a gun from his shroud to point at the cage.

Hank's eyes went wide, but Eduardo put the gun back into his shroud. "I know they're only animals, Hank. That doesn't mean I want them around."

Hank complained, "Uritichs put them here for some reason. We should figure out why."

"Figure it out somewhere else. I'm going on a trip to Lake Havasu. I should be back in two weeks and I want these things gone."

Episode 6 – Protection

As a convoy assembled for the run to Lake Havasu, Eduardo felt better than he had in a long time. Securitas was three hundred strong, Eduardo had managed to keep Dejovine and Wylie apart, Hank's ridiculous effort to scare him with aergels had fallen flat, and he was about to put into place his plan to become the first warlord of Arizona. All it would take was the fall of one major city.

Eduardo would take all three hundred Securitas soldiers to Lake Havasu. Camp Verde was left relatively undefended with only GGC guards and a few dozen Los Diablos who weren't out with convoys. Eduardo expected an argument but Hank Wylie didn't seem to mind. Did he have another army coming, or maybe he really believed in Eduardo's protection scheme?

The convoy pulled onto West Angus Drive where Eduardo waited with Dejovine and a few of his JD Arms salesmen who arrived in the middle of the night. With a pickup truck, garbage truck, three heavy maintenance trucks, and four school buses packed with soldiers, it would be the largest convoy the gulag had ever seen. Even in his excitement to get started, Eduardo didn't overlook the auto trailer pulled by Dejovine's men.

"What's that?"

Dejovine looked up from his cat. "The weapons I'm trying to sell to El Jefe."

"No flamethrowers, right?"

"As agreed, Securitas has exclusive rights to the throwers. We better get moving."

Eduardo didn't budge as Dejovine headed for the JD pickup truck. "What are those then?"

JD men lifted lumpy canvas bags into the back of the pickup truck. "Thermite... iron oxide and powdered aluminum."

"Bombs?"

"It's used for welding heavy metal pieces together. Thermite burns very hot while throwing out blobs of burning iron."

"That could be used against us."

"That's the idea, remember? I'm sure the satchels are no match for your flamethrowers."

Eduardo nodded. "You'll ride with me to Lake Havasu. We'll split up at the airport."

Dejovine typed instructions to JD Arms, and followed Eduardo to one of the big maintenance trucks. Dejovine climbed into the back alone while Eduardo met Ricky and Roberto for last minute instructions. After the inventory of drugs and gas cylinders, Eduardo climbed into the truck with Dejovine. He had more questions about thermite.

As the convoy rolled off, Eduardo grabbed at a railing for support. His hand hit an invisible wall, and he went rolling to the bed. Dejovine pulled him up, helping him to the bench seat against the side.

Eduardo detected a faint glistening of the air on Dejovine's other side. "Who's that?"

"Just a bodyguard."

"I've been out of the pen long enough to know a girl when I bump into one."

"There are female bodyguards. That's just Rafferty."

"Let me see her!"

"I'm afraid not," Dejovine said, but the bodyguard opaqued to reveal a slender figure in silver.

Dejovine said, "Rafferty doesn't speak out loud. She was traumatized on landing day."

"She follows you everywhere?"

"Pretty much."

"That's how you spotted me that first day in Lake Havasu! You have a spy!"

Dejovine chuckled. "You wouldn't believe how many times Rafferty has saved me."

"Yes, I would." Eduardo leaned over. "So, Rafferty, how many times have people spotted you?"

The bodyguard faded without answering. Dejovine said, "Not very often. Rafferty has become very adept at being invisible."

"Practice," Eduardo said. "I have got to get my own invisible bodyguard."

As the convoy roared up Highway 17, Dejovine changed the subject. "So you'll go in first to deliver the gas and drugs."

"*After* we station flamethrowers around the perimeter."

"And then you try to sell protection services to the city."

"A modest monthly surcharge on the city budget."

"But you don't think El Jefe will pay?"

"He will after we burn a few buildings."

"Then we come in to sell thermite and six-shooters at vastly inflated prices."

"Presented with two bad choices, El Jefe will pay for a protection suite, and buy your arms as well to protect Lake Havasu from Securitas."

From Highway 17, the convoy cut west to the 40. Eduardo swooned in waves of déjà vu. Why did he keep going back to Lake Havasu? Was it unfinished business? A chance to fix past mistakes?

Eduardo had been given opportunities to start a family with Maria, be a salesman for JD Arms, provide security for the GGC. Why had Eduardo rejected those lives for a chance to be Warlord? All great figures in history must have rejected smaller, comfortable lives.

There was a chance that El Jefe would figure out what was going on. Certainly he would sniff out the protection racquet. Whether he could do anything about it was the question. Securitas teams with flamethrowers would be mobile and a deadly threat on his doorstep. The additional complexity with JD Arms would hopefully keep El Jefe too unbalanced to mount an effective defense.

When they reached the airport, Eduardo took Roberto to his old office inside the hangar. "Roberto, I have a critical assignment for you. I need a trusted bodyguard here in Lake Havasu."

"Sure, Eduardo, no problem."

"The only thing is, you have to stay invisible."

"Pardon?"

"No one would even know you were there until your services were required."

"I don't get it. When would I opaque?"

"You would stay invisible twenty-four, seven. People would forget there ever was a Roberto. That's the point. They would let down their guard and say things behind my back that you could pick up."

"Seems kind of creepy."

"That is also the point. I'm having a meeting with Dejovine in a few minutes. Just try it out to see how it goes."

Roberto shrugged, and tapped on the screen until he faded from the room. Eduardo said, "Good man. Now just follow at a short distance and keep a hand near your gun. I'll shout if I need help."

Eduardo walked out of the hangar to find Dejovine. If anyone noticed that he came out of the office alone, no one said anything.

Dejovine was at the pickup truck with JD Arms transferring bags of incendiaries to the auto trailer. "Jim, I've had a chance to think. You can take the six-shooters to El Jefe, but Securitas will hold on to the thermite."

JD salesmen kept loading but there was more deliberate thought to their movements. "What for?"

"Maybe the throwers won't be enough. We could use a few fire bombs."

"That wasn't the plan. El Jefe has six-shooters; they aren't going to pay for more. I told him we were bringing thermite."

"If you hold it back, he will pay that much more. Just tell him that it's on its way. When

Securitas has signed the contract we'll give you back the thermite."

"He'll kill us!"

"El Jefe isn't like that. You'll be fine, and that is my final decision. Just load the thermite bags into one of our school buses."

Eduardo braced himself to call Roberto into action. Dejovine hesitated only moments. "Okay, Eduardo. I hope you know what you're doing. Guys?"

As JD men redirected the canvas bags, Eduardo looked slowly around the parking lot for Roberto. Just knowing that his invisible bodyguard/assassin was there increased his confidence. Now where was Rafferty? Presumably she was in the lot as well.

Securitas drove slowly around the outskirts of Lake Havasu. In hills and deserts they stationed teams with flamethrowers. Roberto's absence was explained away as a secret assignment. The few who caught the glint of Eduardo's new shadow didn't say anything. Even they would forget eventually. Roberto complained only through Eduardo's cat of his growing loneliness.

When all was ready, two maintenance trucks from the convoy drove into town. They would meet El Jefe at his headquarters while the majority of men and material was held back. The deal for barter, gas, and drugs had already been negotiated by radio, but Eduardo was sure that he could piggyback his protection services.

With Roberto lurking, Eduardo welcomed the sense of déjà vu as he was led into El Jefe's reception area once again. It was a little concerning that a security dog didn't alert to the spy. Maybe it was there only for show, or maybe Roberto got boxed out in the hallway.

Again, El Jefe didn't seem to recognize Eduardo as his aide made introductions. El Jefe said, "I'm not sure what we're doing here? Haven't the details already been worked out?"

The aide cleared his throat. "El Jefe, Eduardo requested this meeting to discuss additional services offered through the GGC."

El Jefe focused on Eduardo's face. "You were here before."

"I landed at Lake Havasu, and ran red group for some weeks. I know La Fuerza, and I know the city. I think we could guard your borders and keep the city safe."

"We haven't been attacked yet; the closest cities don't even have militias."

As El Jefe rose from the sofa, Eduardo said, "Town militias aren't the only threat. The eastern cities are catching slaves, and there are rumors of a state army forming in Phoenix."

El Jefe didn't react. As he was led slowly away, Eduardo added, "I would hate to see your neighborhoods burned."

El Jefe turned. "I would hate to see the deal blown up and your goods confiscated."

Eduardo wasn't worried about the threat; that is how negotiations worked. "Securitas wouldn't allow that. I could show you the awesome firepower at our disposal. These same weapons can be used in your service. It would only require a small monthly charge to the city…"

"Mr. Dios! My aides report that you have only a few dozen soldiers. I doubt they could have weapons of any size that could challenge Lake Havasu's forces."

As El Jefe headed for the hallway, Eduardo shouted, "This negotiation isn't over!"

Ricky yelled from the window, "Eduardo! They're taking the trucks!"

Inside the reception area, La Fuerza guards pulled guns from their shrouds. The aide said, "Leave quietly and the barter will be handed over at the border."

Eduardo raged at the concession; they would still honor the deal! Even with Securitas trucks in La Fuerza's control, El Jefe wouldn't crush his opposition. "Roberto! Kill El Jefe! Ricky, call the reserves! Fight to the trucks!"

Securitas pulled hammers and guns from shrouds. The German Shepherd galloped across the room and leapt for an invisible figure. Roberto fought back, rolling over the yapping dog. He was safe enough, but trapped inside his shroud, he couldn't bring out a hammer to slam El Jefe in the head.

Eduardo pushed the aide over a chair while gunshots filled the room with smoke and flash. Eduardo followed Ricky for the hallway as the outnumbered but more experienced Securitas soldiers battled hand to hand.

By the time they reached the lobby door, the two sides were fully engaged outside as well. One of the maintenance trucks was burning, and flame blew out from Securitas throwers crouched in the bed.

The thermite was dispersed with teams outside of town. Eduardo didn't know if methane cylinders in the truck would blow up but he wasn't going to wait around to find out. He turned invisible and ran for a sandy ditch to follow the battle on his cat. Ricky gave orders for a relief team hiding in Wheeler Park to come pull them out. Other flamethrower teams were too far away to reach them in time.

Eduardo cursed himself for bringing so few soldiers to the meeting. El Jefe didn't take them seriously, but things might work out better this way. The concessions he could have wrung from El Jefe would have been small. Securitas would squeeze them now. The price would be grossly higher, and El Jefe wouldn't fail to recognize him next time.

Surviving Securitas soldiers fought free of the Medical Complex. They turned invisible, and made their way through city neighborhoods to a rally point on the beach two kilometers away. As they trickled in, Eduardo took inventory. They had lost thirty soldiers and half of the drugs and methane cylinders. Roberto made it out as well, although he had to jump out a second story window to do it.

With flamethrowers, thermite, and two hundred and seventy soldiers, Securitas sealed off the city north and south along Highway 95. The lake was impassible to the west. Mountains and several hundred kilometers of baking desert stretched to the east. The city was his, but Eduardo was no richer.

Residents sealed inside shrouds could get away at any time, but few took advantage. Most of them had never even heard about Securitas, only rumors of a fight at the Medical Complex. Except for the drafting of a few extra bangers from each gang, life inside their neighborhoods continued as before.

Securitas teams in camouflage snuck into town. To hold La Fuerza's attention, they started small fires while JD Arms drove in with the six-shooters to sell.

Jim Dejovine was gone four days. He refused repeated calls over the cat radio. Had Dejovine betrayed Securitas, or was he being held captive by El Jefe? The map screen on the cat showed JD dots in and around the hospital. They hadn't shut off their shared location data, so Eduardo was left to wonder what was going on.

There was a problem laying siege to a city inside the gulag. With shrouds producing food, water, and shelter, residents were self-sufficient. Major routes into and out of Lake Havasu had been sealed off, but dogs patrolled the border. It was harder and harder to insert teams for sabotage, and Securitas lost a few more men each day.

While waiting for a strike force to return from the marijuana farm, a voice came over the emergency channel, "Ricky, are you up?"

Sitting in the airport hangar with Eduardo and other officers, Ricky thumbed his cat. "Yeah, Jon, go ahead."

"There's a spaceship headed north."

"A spaceship?"

"Rockets, fire… could be some kind of troop transport. It could be headed for the airport."

"Did El Jefe send it?"

"I don't think so. This is massive."

Eduardo and the other Securitas officers walked outside the hangar. In darkened skies long yellow-red flames danced on the horizon like genies. Ricky said, "Should we evacuate?"

Eduardo shook his head. "HIGS, do you have a spaceship in Lake Havasu?"

"Yes, Eduardo, the quad-lifter is delivering an extraction point."

"Delivering where?"

"To the Lake Havasu airport."

Eduardo looked at Ricky. "This may be our key. Do we still have the thermite?"

"What are you going to do?"

"El Jefe may not care about a few neighborhoods, but we can threaten to burn down their way out of the gulag."

"That's our way out too."

"There are other extraction points. Call in our teams. In the morning there will be curious residents coming from the city."

Thirty meters to a side, the extraction point was a shining, seamless metal cube ten-stories tall. Slung under the belly, the massive quad-lifter lowered it to the ground in between the airport and city. The roar of rockets at each of the four corners shook the walls of the hangar and echoed off rock hills. There certainly would be a few curious townies heading out to look.

After the cube was set firmly at the edge of a runway access road, the lifter detached and rose again without ever fully shutting off the rockets. Eduardo and the others jogged out into the night to touch it, but silvery metal insects the size of refrigerators rolled out of sliding panels at the base.

Eduardo said, "HIGS, what are those robots?"

"They are called 'defenders', Eduardo, and they will not let you burn down the extraction cube."

"You were eavesdropping?"

"I listen through every cat in the gulag. I didn't have to warn you; I could have let the defenders take care of it their way."

"Which is?"

"Metal slugs accelerated to the speed of sound."

A few of the most daring soldiers walked gently past defenders to touch the cube. "It's talking to my suit!" one shouted in amazement.

Cons pressed their backs to metal walls but none were pulled inside. They had months or years yet to run on their sentences. Standing a hundred meters away with Eduardo, Ricky said, "Should I still gather the thermite?"

"Yes, bring it. El Jefe won't know we can't burn the cube down."

Securitas tried to keep townies away, but the curious were increasingly violent and persistent. After losing another half-dozen soldiers, Eduardo pulled Securitas back and let the townies in. A few were even pulled inside the cube to the astonishment of everyone.

A week after the beginning of the ineffectual siege, Jim Dejovine called Eduardo. Waiting glumly in the airport hangar, Eduardo startled at the crackling of his cat radio. "Jim? What's going on?"

"I think our plan will work."

"El Jefe's going to sign a protection contract?"

"Oh no, he would never do that. El Jefe wants the thermite."

"Excuse me? I threatened to burn down the extraction cube with it."

Dejovine laughed. "I know, he told me. I finally told him you and I were working together."

"Why would he let you live?"

"For the thermite, and future deliveries of flamethrowers. You don't need a protection racquet, Eduardo. You can make far more barter helping me make and sell arms through the company."

Eduardo had been a salesman before; it was too much like begging. He wanted an army; he wanted cities paying him to keep the peace. Whatever Eduardo decided, it would have to be soon; Securitas was getting restless. "There's another option. You could have Rafferty assassinate El Jefe. You're sleeping in the same building, aren't you?"

"That's out of the question. Rafferty's just a kid. She's not an assassin."

"She was in prison, wasn't she? What was she in for?"

"I don't know, but this is not an option."

Eduardo sighed. "Okay, Jim, it's a deal. I'll send a school bus with the thermite to El Jefe's hospital. In exchange I want all the barter that was promised before plus a hundred kilos of pot."

"I think he'll go for that."

After Eduardo cut the connection, the relief on Ricky's face was comical. Eduardo clucked his tongue. "Not so fast, Ricky. Load bags of thermite onto a school bus and rig it with a fuse."

"A fuse, Eduardo?"

"El Jefe is being unreasonable. Whether he dies in the blast or not, his successor, or a wounded El Jefe, will be easier to deal with."

Ricky sighed. "Yes, Eduardo. Should I warn Dejovine?"

"Dejovine made his bed inside El Jefe's compound. Let him wake up with fleas."

Technicians from the JD Arms Company could have built a time-delay fuse with a battery and kitchen timer. No one in Securitas had that expertise, and HIGS wouldn't help. Eduardo settled for a dynamite wick burning at a rate of ten minutes per meter. With six bags of thermite, a fourth of their supply, a school bus set off from the airport with a single driver.

The bus was expected and passed along through checkpoints. The driver parked it as close to El Jefe's hospital as he could get, lit the fuse, and walked off the bus in camo to get away invisibly through the city. Back at the airport, Eduardo learned of the result as a rumble through the ground, followed by a loud boom and black column of smoke.

Eduardo looked casually at the locator map on his cat. A blinking light indicated Dejovine's cat still lived. It remained to be seen whether Dejovine lived or was cooked inside his suit. Eduardo couldn't imagine he wouldn't have immediately gone outside to secure the thermite.

The driver of the bus called. "Ricky, it's Saul. The package was delivered."

"No kidding. We saw a small mushroom cloud."

"The building was ripped open and fires continue inside."

"Casualties?"

"I see a few dozen bodies. The shrouds are great insulation but they can be overwhelmed by a hot enough fire."

Eduardo said, "Do you know if El Jefe still lives?"

"They're still staggering out of the back half of the building. Do you want me to try and find out?"

"Yes, please, and Dejovine as well."

When the radio clicked off, Ricky said, "I guess you got their attention."

"Their attention is only a small part of what I want. Have the rest of the thermite dispersed with the flamethrower teams. If we don't get the protection contract in the next twenty-four hours I'm going to burn down the city."

Before the Securitas driver was able to identify survivors, Jim Dejovine called. "I must admit I didn't see this coming, Eduardo."

"You gave me little choice. I hope Rafferty is all right as well."

"We were both deep inside the building, thank you. Thank you also for not using the entire thermite supply in your bomb."

"How do you know that wasn't all of it?"

"From the size of the blast, my engineer estimated it was only a third."

"A fourth actually. I just wanted to send a message."

"Well, your message was received. El Jefe survived. He will sign the protection contract with Securitas."

Eduardo thought back on all the times El Jefe had rejected him. "That's no longer enough, Jim. I need to know El Jefe is serious."

"What do you want? Another hundred kilos of pot?"

"What is that to him? No, I want Randall's head delivered here to the airport."

A long silence followed. Ricky mouthed, "Eduardo, no!"

Dejovine answered finally, "Are you sure? Who is Randall?"

"El Jefe will know. You have until three o'clock tomorrow."

"For the answer of the head?"

"They're the same thing, Jim. See you soon."

After Eduardo cut the channel, Ricky wailed, "Eduardo, why?"

The demand had been impulsive, but Eduardo liked it the more he thought about it. El Jefe would be humiliated. Would he really deliver Randall's head? At this point it didn't really matter. Eduardo missed out seeing the explosion at the hospital. He wouldn't mind seeing the whole city burn.

When Securitas split apart in Lake Havasu, Hispanics mostly went with Eduardo to Camp Verde, and Blacks mostly stayed with Randall. Among foot soldiers there were no hard feelings, just choice and individual calculations. Securitas Hispanics had nothing against Randall, so Ricky didn't tell them about Eduardo's demand. There was almost zero chance that El Jefe would actually agree.

At sunrise the next morning, a car drove out slowly from town. Ricky didn't make the connection until he saw a body wrapped in the back seat. Heart sinking to his stomach, Ricky told a lieutenant, "Go wake Eduardo."

"Who's that?"

"Now."

La Fuerza's deliveryman kept the engine running. He dragged the body onto the asphalt, nodded to Ricky, and climbed back into the car. As a few other early risers gathered around the body, Ricky said, "Help me carry him to the office."

"Who is it?"

"I'm not one hundred percent sure," Ricky said truthfully.

"Shouldn't we unwrap him and see?"

Ricky snapped, "I don't think Eduardo would appreciate that."

Pall bearers took the hint. They carried the body into the office as Eduardo was just arriving. Ricky shooed the others out and let Eduardo call the next step. He knelt and ran a hand over the blanket. "Randall?"

"We didn't unwrap and the driver didn't say."

Eduardo gripped the edge of the blanket and lifted. A Black man rolled onto the ground. Ending in a face-up position, he appeared to be in his early thirties. In death, Eduardo couldn't be sure, but Ricky's hard swallow confirmed the identity. "I asked only for the head. I'm not sure this meets my demand."

"Oh, Eduardo no," Ricky pleaded.

"Did you tell anyone who this is?"

"No. We can just bury him and not say anything."

"Why would we do that?"

"A lot of our people liked Randall."

"So did I... I respected him anyway."

Ricky looked astonished. "Then why?"

"Because it weakens El Jefe in front of his people."

"Maybe they don't even know."

"Huh?"

Ricky hooked a thumb to the door. "It's barely light outside. La Fuerza probably kidnapped

Randall last night in his sleep. It wouldn't be hard in camo. Maybe Randall's gang doesn't even know he's gone."

Eduardo's eyes hardened. "El Jefe is spitting in my eye! He thinks he found a loophole."

"What are you going to do?"

"Call in the men. We're going to burn the city down."

"Eduardo, no! They won't do it!"

"They will when they see what El Jefe did to Randall."

Eduardo pretended indecision in front of his men. He let their anger boil while summer days grew hot enough to melt the city without thermite. When he woke one morning to a dry wind blowing over the desert, Eduardo knew it was time to move.

Teams were already in place around the perimeter. With thirty-six throwers they would advance on the city: from the airport heading south, Highway 95 heading north, the desert mountain roads heading west and all along the river heading inland. Havasuvians would be trapped in a box like rats.

Despite Ricky's prediction, few of the Securitas foot soldiers raised objections. They had been fighting so long, Eduardo had the feral army he wanted.

To maximize the heat, Eduardo scheduled his holocaust for one p.m. Dry winds blowing throughout the day were a good omen. As Securitas soldiers waited, they watched shows on their cats, and stayed alert for any signs of an exodus.

Sitting at the airport, Eduardo received reports of a few boats heading south on the lake. Someone in Securitas had warned ex-colleagues in Randall's gang. Eduardo would like to know who, but word didn't seem to have gone beyond that one small group.

Eduardo ate from his cat. At noon he gathered with Ricky and a group of twenty soldiers. El Jefe still thought they had a deal: gas, drugs, and protection for barter. Eduardo would like to see the look on his face when smoke started rising from every direction. For the second time, Dejovine was kept in the dark.

After the operation, Securitas would leave Lake Havasu in a much-reduced convoy. Eduardo had vehicles loaded with gas from the cylinders. Soldiers would be coming back in a hurry and might possibly be fighting a rearguard action.

Ricky would coordinate the operation. As final orders were sent out, Eduardo turned on his camo and walked alone towards town. He checked the clock on the cat and switched among radio channels.

Wisps of smoke blew above the southern end of the lake. Five minutes early, maybe the team had been detected by patrols. If even a half of the teams were successful, Lake Havasu should be destroyed.

Eduardo passed Chenoweth Drive bordering a luxury neighborhood separated from town. He passed Lake Drive bordering a working class neighborhood, and stopped at the Falls Spring Wash Bridge. A few hundred meters from the sprawling town proper, it was as close as he dared to get. The first ropes of flame lashed out and dropped on the outermost houses like a wave.

Not expecting attack, La Fuerza's armies had gone home. Gangs inhabiting the neighborhoods would either run or fight back with the few weapons at their disposal. The toughest defenders would be hit with thermite bombs blowing out chunks of concrete and molten iron.

Eduardo peeked over the bridge railing. Residents in shining metal suits ran screaming out of the flames. Orange walls grew taller and crawled over rows of houses like giant orange worms. Eduardo could no longer see the yellow-white whips of his throwers, but the popping of thermite bombs echoed around the city.

At some point the fire grew beyond the men feeding it. She became a living thing, circling the city faster and faster to catch her tail. As she rose into the tornado sky, residents in shrouds could stand the heat for only so long. If they didn't get out early they weren't getting out.

Eduardo rose on shaky legs. He staggered back to the airport as the voices of some of his own burning men screamed over the radio. Eduardo switched off completely, sweating silently inside his shroud.

Securitas soldiers waited by the convoy to whisk him away from the carnage. If Eduardo could feel any guilt at all, it was reflected off the mirrored side of the extraction cube, a burning city turning to ash.

Eduardo had very little to show for the convoy he took to Lake Havasu. The drugs were gone, the protection contract was burned to a crisp, and all the gas they could save had been transferred into the vehicles they had left. On the plus side, Securitas still had a hundred and fifty soldiers, and they had the entire gulag living in fear for their lives.

Eduardo expected little further resistance. Securitas split into three groups to extract protection contracts from Topock, Bullhead City, and Kingman. Eduardo and Ricky split off from the convoy at Topock with thirty soldiers.

The closest to Lake Havasu, and with a pre-gulag population of 1400, Topock was the smallest, and should fold quickly. They could then roll up the cities all the way to Flagstaff, and then down to Camp Verde to reload on gas and drugs.

The burning of Lake Havasu was no secret. Skies darkened over much of the state. Floating ash provided spectacular orange-purple sunsets. If cons didn't hear screams of friends over their cat radios, they may have heard stories from some of the five thousand who escaped the furnace. Fifty kilometers away, residents of Topock saw even the fire tornado scouring streets and the sandy washes of Lake Havasu.

On the border of the Colorado River there was only one road into Topock. In a single long school bus, Securitas rolled into the Shell station on Golden Shores Parkway.

Eduardo waited for a representative to come surrender the town. Havasuvians walking in through the desert would surely testify to the savagery of Securitas, but no town authority arrived to negotiate. Maybe Topock had no mayor or town council.

Securitas soldiers sent to find someone in charge were met by snipers or tools swung by invisible fists. After a few days, Eduardo began to get annoyed. He sat with Ricky inside the gas station market. "You need to get them to fear us."

Ricky sucked on a hard candy. "Flamethrowers and thermite bombs are gone. We're just thirty bandits sitting out by the gas station. Do you think we could get more gas out of Camp Verde?"

"We're still security for the GGC. I'll give Hank a call."

"There's something you should know. Jim Dejovine made it out of Lake Havasu. He's in Camp Verde now."

"I guess Jim and Hank finally got together. Maybe we'll get some more thermite out of this."

"You think Dejovine would do anything for us after we tried to burn him in Lake Havasu?"

"Securitas still has more foot soldiers than the GGC and Los Diablos."

When Ricky looked uncomfortable, Eduardo prodded. "What?"

"It may just be a rumor, but I heard that Dejovine is trying to raise a new militia. They're called Rangers."

Eduardo snapped his fingers. "Roberto."

Ricky jumped when his old lieutenant materialized at his elbow. Ricky grabbed his shoulders. "I thought you got killed in Lake Havasu!"

Eduardo grinned. "Imagine Hank's surprise when Roberto shows up next to *him*."

Roberto said, "Eduardo?"

"You're no longer my bodyguard. I need somebody inside the room when I call Hank. If things don't go my way, I'll need you to take him out."

When Roberto left, Ricky said, "What do we do about Topock?"

"Recall the team from Bullhead City. We need more bodies here. We may not be able to burn the town, but we can take out resistance block by block."

Topockans had little reason to defend a town they didn't even own in the first place, but stiffened by angry Havasuvians, townspeople continued to fight back.

It took Roberto five days to reach Camp Verde and worm his way into position. In that time, thirty soldiers arrived from Bullhead City to help break Topock. Eduardo had to move quickly now or give up the idea altogether. In a foul mood, he called Hank to get help. "Hey, partner."

"Eduardo, can you wait a minute while I send for Pedro?"

"Sure, Hank, this will concern the GGC as well." Eduardo had to stifle a laugh. Standing invisibly inside the gas shed with Hank, Roberto texted back, [Pedro is going to get Dejovine.]

Stalling for time, Hank said, "How's every little thing?"

"Can't complain. Our plans are proceeding on schedule."

"*Our* plans?"

"We're negotiating security contracts with Kingman, Topock, and Bullhead City."

"Here's Pedro."

Roberto texted, [Pedro is back with Jim.]

[Watch out for Jim's invisible bodyguard Rafferty.]

Pedro said, "Hi, Eduardo. Long time, no hear. What's happening?"

"We're running low on supplies. I need you to run another convoy up here with about two kilos of fent and a hundred cylinders of methane."

Hank said, "We're short on buses, Eduardo. It could take a while."

"Are you sure you're not loading them with Rangers?"

Pedro said, "Securitas has been doing so well up north, we're building a similar force to head south."

"Hah! Rangers are filled with rats escaped from our traps. I need those supplies, Hank. If you can't send them, we'll come take them ourselves."

"Do you think that you could?"

Eduardo laughed. "You think Rangers will save you, Hank? We've got the most experienced fighters inside the gulag. Even with Jim's weapons, Securitas will chew your boys up for breakfast."

Roberto texted, [That shook him up! He didn't know you knew about Dejovine!]

Eduardo might get the supplies after all. "We're still partners, Hank. It doesn't have to be this way. I know you're mad about Lake Havasu, but that was personal. I wouldn't burn another city."

"You wouldn't?"

"Of course not. We have the same goals, a gulag-wide organization of drugs, transportation, and above all safety. We'll outlaw slavery and take on the gangs. What do you say, Hank? If Rangers joined with Securitas, not even Tucson or Phoenix could resist."

Hank sighed. "Could I call you in the morning?"

"Sure, Hank, sleep tight."

When the radio disconnected, Eduardo typed frantically, [Turn on your radio. I need to hear.]

Thinking they were alone, Dejovine said, "You're actually considering his offer? We have over a thousand men to Eduardo's three hundred, and who knows how many he lost in Lake Havasu… maybe half."

"You've seen Securitas fight. Could you guarantee a Ranger victory?"

When Dejovine hesitated, Hank said, "That's what I thought. Let me sleep on it. Let's all sleep on it, and we'll talk again in the morning before we call Eduardo. Pedro, are the Rangers ready to go?"

"Horse soldiers could hit Topock in two days. Foot soldiers could reach Topock, Bullhead City, and Kingman in a week."

"Okay, let's keep this discussion between us for now. The entire future direction of the gulag could be decided in the next week."

After Pedro and Dejovine walked out, Hank bolted the door. Eduardo texted to Roberto, [We can't let Hank send the Rangers against us.]

[Hank said they would decide in the morning.]

[We can't take that chance. I know you don't want to do it, but you got to take him out tonight. Leave your radio on. I want to hear.]

Roberto waited an hour to make sure Hank's partners wouldn't return. Soft snores filled the channel as Roberto made his move, and then Hank's startled scream was cut off quickly by the garrote.

The sounds of fighting continued long after the time Hank should have succumbed. A metal tool slammed repeatedly into a shroud, crunching photocells and breaking capillaries or bones underneath.

Hank finally croaked, "Rafferty... Who?"

Eduardo's blood turned to ice. Dejovine's invisible bodyguard had stayed behind. Stupid Roberto! Eduardo raged at his feckless assassin, but he listened closely as Roberto's radio continued to transmit.

There was a hammering on the door, and Pedro's voice, "Hank! It's me! Open up!"

The door bolt slid. Hank tried to mumble an explanation while Dejovine ran in, shouting, "Rafferty! Where are you?" Seconds later, he said, "Did he talk?"

A pipe scraped across the floor. Dejovine said, "Pedro, bolt the door."

After the mute Rafferty's explanation through text, Hank said, "How can I ever repay you for my life?"

Pedro said, "I guess Eduardo didn't want to wait for an answer. Jim and I would have found you dead in the morning and called off the whole operation."

"But the gas and drugs would be cut off."

"Eduardo's working on a new model. Why go through the hassle of organizing convoys when you can be a warlord?"

Pedro said, "Do we tell Eduardo that we stopped his assassin? We could take the cat away and keep him tied up in camp. Eduardo wouldn't know we're coming."

Dejovine said, "He has other spies besides this one. The assassination attempt was a gambit to win everything in a single strike. Even if it failed, this is Eduardo's declaration to us. We're at war, gentlemen."

Eduardo heard the sounds of Roberto's hood being unzipped. Before he could beg for mercy, Roberto's voice drowned in a gurgle of blood. Eduardo was shaken as the radio signal drained out along with Roberto's life. Which of the three men had the stomach to stab a man in the throat?

Before the call, Eduardo considered pardoning Topock if they just signed a no-fee protection contract. It would be worth it just to disengage and move on to the next city. After Roberto's killing, Hank would need a further demonstration of Eduardo's power. Topock would have to be emptied of residents or destroyed.

Securitas set up barracks at the Golden Shores Community Center. At the edge of town along Oatman Highway, Securitas would force Topockans to the river. Lake Havasu to the south was destroyed. Refugees would have to run north to Bullhead City or east towards Kingman. Securitas would be right on their heels.

A week passed since Roberto's failed attempt to assassinate Hank Wylie. Units of the newly formed Rangers had still not arrived. They were either having trouble getting started or Hank decided not to send them after all.

Eduardo lost his caution, demanding Ricky send more of their soldiers into town. Late in the morning, Ricky heard the sounds of hoof beats before he saw the clouds of dust rising along Highway 10. Climbing from the roof where he maintained an observation post, Ricky yelled, "Eduardo, camo!"

The first Ranger units to reach Topock did more scouting than fighting. Hanging outside of town, hit and run raids tied down Securitas, keeping them from heading back to Camp Verde. Eduardo knew what Rangers were doing, but as long as losses were light, he couldn't give up the idea of punishing Topock.

In every skirmish or small battle, Securitas came out on top. Time and again, Ranger cavalry or foot soldiers were forced to retreat, but their numbers never seemed to diminish. For every body lying in the streets of Topock, two more arrived from Camp Verde. Ricky argued for disengagement, but their gas was gone, and the ammo running out. A strategic retreat would be seen for the defeat it was.

Eduardo heard rumors of a new project at Camp Verde that might offer him a way out. Hank Wylie tapped a crude oil pipeline, and they were making gasoline. Every armed gang in the gulag would want in on that. Hank needed the Rangers that were being thrown against him in Topock.

He called impulsively. "Hey, partner, you never called back about those supplies."

"I got a sore throat all of a sudden."

Eduardo laughed. "You returned the favor. That was cold-blooded."

"What do you mean?"

"I didn't think you capable of stabbing a bound man in the throat."

"Where did you hear that?"

"Roberto's radio was on. I was listening the whole time. That was a ghastly death rattle as he took a last breath. Tell me who placed the stroke, you, Jim, or Pedro?"

"That is none of your business, and consider our partnership dissolved."

"What for?"

"Trying to kill me for one."

"Apparently that was the problem; I should have sent two. I didn't take you for a fighter. After Roberto took you out I was going to break off up here and get the home office in order."

"What changed your mind?"

"You did, Hank, with that blade in Roberto's throat. I realized you were strong enough to defend the place from outsiders."

"You mean defend it from you. Don't act like a master tactician. You're stuck up north, and now the Rangers will hunt you down."

"I'll admit they give me trouble. Is it worth weakening both forces when we would be so much stronger as allies?"

"You're unbelievable. You waited too long to act, and now you're stuck. You only called to beg for your life."

"Okay, Hank, you keep thinking that. I wanted to buy some of that new gasoline of yours. If you're going to be an ass, I'll just come get it myself." Eduardo's threat was only a bluff. From the increasing numbers of Rangers hitting them, there was no way Securitas could match them in battle.

Over the next week, Securitas' offensive war against Topock turned into a defensive stand against both Rangers and emboldened citizens. By mid-December, Securitas was reduced to ten soldiers struggling to hold onto the community center at the edge of town.

After a random gunshot, Ricky peered through a hole into the darkness. He no longer had to climb to his observation post. Ranger missiles tore view ports into the sides of the building. Sitting on his cot, Eduardo said, "How's it look?"

"Nothing to get excited about. Our patrols would have reported any larger movement."

"So? You better get some sleep."

"I heard from Ralph that it's snowing in Flagstaff."

The suit kept his body warm, but Eduardo's uncowled breath sent clouds of condensation. "Looks like we'll have a white Christmas after all."

"I was thinking that if we left town now, we could get out without leaving footprints."

When Eduardo didn't immediately take offense, Ricky knew he was beaten. Eduardo said wistfully, "After Lake Havasu, any city in America would have paid protection. Cons are just too stupid."

"No, they're stubborn... and they don't have much to lose. What are we going to do, Eduardo?"

"What do you think we should do?"

"I talked with the boys. They'd like to stay together as a group. Should we head back to Camp Verde?"

"Hank wouldn't have us, and there are too many Rangers to dislodge. We'll be lucky to get away from the ones they sent here."

"Rangers can't track ghosts... unless we leave footprints."

"I get it, you want out. Name a destination."

"Well... you're the boss, Eduardo."

A patrol in camo knocked and crunched through glass in the smashed entryway. They opaqued and unzipped hoods. Juan said, "What's going on?"

"Ricky and I were deciding where to go next. Any ideas?"

"I have a cousin living in Show Low. He hunts runaway slaves for their farms."

Eduardo looked to Ricky who shrugged. Eduardo nodded thoughtfully. "We could keep doing what we love. Ricky, call the men in Kingman. Juan, call your cousin. If Show Low doesn't need another team of hunters, some other slave city will."

Episode 7 – The Palace

Remnants of Securitas gathered in a small town on the eastern side of Flagstaff. Winona was barely a truck stop on the way to Winslow, but it provided a surprising number of luxurious houses scattered around the highland scrub desert. In advance of Eduardo's arrival, Securitas lieutenants secured a large two-story house hidden in the hills on Parson Ranch Road.

The men were in surprisingly good spirits as Eduardo and Ricky stepped through the front door. Finding his hands immediately busy with a joint and a bottle of wine, Eduardo allowed a few moments of gratitude before crafting his next words.
"Gentlemen! Survivors! Congratulations on proving yourselves the best!"

The audience drank sloppily to the sentiment. Crowding the living room, dining room, kitchen and hallways, they seemed more numerous than the fifty that Ricky tracked in his lists, fifty out of the three hundred who left Camp Verde. Where had it gone wrong?

"Our attempts to bring security to cities of the gulag may have fallen short, but we won't give up the vision. To those of you who haven't heard, tomorrow we head east to the slave cities. We'll take over security in Show Low on our way to building a new empire!"

As the men cheered, Eduardo added, "We'll take only what we can carry, so finish off your luxuries tonight!"

Eduardo stuck around long enough to be polite. He talked with men he hadn't seen in many weeks. Sharing drugs and stories, he tried not to shudder at disfiguring injuries. As quickly as possible Eduardo went upstairs to a bedroom. He had Ricky put a guard at the door.

Vehicles in both Topock and Kingman had run out of methane. Securitas soldiers would be on foot, hiking the two hundred kilometers to Show Low. Juan had not been able to get in touch with his cousin, but Eduardo assumed they could always use slave hunters. Once Eduardo figured out the set up, they could take over the city easily enough. Despite setbacks and injuries, raucous laughter from downstairs filled Eduardo with confidence.

They took Highway 40 out of town towards Winslow. Soldiers didn't bother with camo. Daring resistance from the dregs of Winona they walked in broad daylight. After fighting so long, Securitas didn't realize that most cons just wanted to be left alone, not that they wouldn't take advantage of an opportunity. Living on the border of slave cities, many of those wary cons had unsavory contacts.

After two days walking, they saw no sign of travelers on the vast open sands. Securitas took over the Winslow Fire Department at the edge of town. With Securitas expecting to find work shortly, the party that began in a house in Winona resumed in Winslow.

With a beer in hand, Eduardo stood at the open roll door of the engine bay. A skinny black lab poked a face around the corner. Eduardo threw his empty can, and laughed as the dog scampered backwards growling.

Suddenly alert, Rick stood and walked to the door. Peering into bright sunlight, he whispered, "Do you hear that?"

Out of beer, Eduardo picked up his joint. Swirling smoke parted in the tendrils of steel whips arcing into the garage like the arms of an octopus. Subject to heroin delusions, it took Eduardo long moments to recognize the attack.

Over the peppered sounds of gunfire was the click of a cable grabbing onto his thigh. Trying to kick it aside, Eduardo stumbled and fell to the ground. He thrashed his leg, but the cable stuck.

With the power of an electromagnet another body was reeled past him. Eduardo fought for his zipper until a body landed on top of him. "Open up and you die!" Taking his breath away, the attacker slammed him on the chest with a pipe. All of Eduardo's many battle injuries responded in concert with the pain in his lungs.

Before Eduardo could respond, the attacker moved further into the building. The cable dragged Eduardo to a refrigerator-sized cart where he joined others fighting the same sticky webs. Bodies rushed past them into the building. Two Securitas captives unzipped and scrambled away naked. Others who tried were beaten with pipes. Eduardo wisely left his fate to time.

When the cart was full of prey, attackers dragged it out to the road. Another took its place and fighting continued inside the building. The whole operation took less than thirty minutes.

Eduardo would have sworn attackers numbered more than a hundred. By the time Securitas was dragged out and strung with wires, less than thirty attackers total were going through their things. Eduardo thought Securitas bangers were tough, but they actually outnumbered their captors.

The heavy cabinets they were cabled to could be pulled down the street, but the attackers stayed on them, striking them with iron bars at any sign of movement. Eduardo yelled for someone in charge until his back and arms were beaten blue.

At sunset a U-Haul trailer was pulled by hand to the Fire Department. Two of the attackers waded in to finally separate Eduardo with a wand inserted into the cabinet. An older Black man sitting inside the Fire Department was speaking with his lieutenants as Eduardo was led in. He dispatched them with a final word, and said to Eduardo, "You wanted to talk?"

Eduardo hated asking for favors, but he had little leverage. "I think there must be some misunderstanding… uh…"

"Carl."

"Carl. My name is Eduardo Dios and my gang was coming to join the slave cities."

"Oh, you'll join us alright."

"I didn't mean as slaves. We'd like to hire out as slave hunters."

"How many dogs you got? Unless you can smell through camo, you aren't much good to us. Listen, Ed, a word of advice, accept your fate. A gulag-wide government is forming in Phoenix. Slavery isn't going to last forever; pick beans for a year or two and you'll be out. Not a bad price to pay for your life."

"Securitas is worth much more than a pail of beans. We're the toughest gang around."

Carl looked to the door and the mass of bodies huddled around the cabinets. "You may be hot stuff in the west, but slave cities are a whole other level."

"Have you heard about the burning of Lake Havasu?"

"That was Securitas? What's your name again?"

"Eduardo Dios."

"Well, Ed, I'll check around. Until then, keep your boys quiet. Normally we'd kill a few on the road home as a warning to the rest."

Eduardo dipped his head in gratitude. "How'd you find us anyway?"

"You should have been more generous with your hosts in Winona. We pay a few rats in the border cities to keep an eye out. They get a bounty."

The slave hunters weren't from Show Low, but a city called St. Johns near the border with New Mexico. Inside their U-Haul trailer they had a hundred pairs of iron shackles. Upon seeing the shackles, Securitas captives traded frantic whispers of revolt.

When Eduardo caught on, he yelled, "Knock it off! I talked with their leader. We'll get our shrouds back in St. Johns."

It was a lie, but the men stopped fighting. In shackles, Salvation Army clothes, and poor fitting shoes, they were made ready to march to captivity. As a final insult, Securitas soldiers had to load the electromagnet cabinets into the U-Haul and pull it back to St. Johns. The hundred and fifty kilometers would take four days, eating from their cats that rode along in the pile of suits.

The dogs had no trouble distinguishing slaves. They trotted possessively around camp and ran off to hunt when opportunities presented. The group traveled Highway 40 bordering the Little Colorado River, crossing bridges and generally heading down to the valley city of Holbrook.

Roads into the slave city were guarded, but the team from St. Johns was passed through. Slavers spent the night in cabins along the way while Securitas captives were left to huddle outside under blankets.

On the third night, Eduardo was shaken awake before dawn. A man whispered, "Are you Eduardo Dios?"

"Who wants to know?"

The man pulled bolt cutters from his shroud, and sliced him out of line. Eduardo resisted the man's pull. "Who are you?"

As Securitas stirred around them, the man said tersely, "I'm a friend of your mother's. I'm taking you to see her."

"Now wait just a minute. I'm not going anywhere." The man snapped out a mailed fist.

Eduardo regained consciousness as sunlight reached over an eastern mountain range. He rubbed his jaw, and looked around the desert clearing. No roads or houses were within sight. "Why'd you do that?"

"You were making too much noise. I paid off the dog handlers, but some of the other St. Johns' slavers wouldn't be happy losing you."

Eduardo sat up in a panic. "My suit! We got to go back!"

The man lit a cigarette and leaned against a rock. "Not going to happen. It's over three hundred klicks to Phoenix, and I got business there."

"What kind of business?"

"The Constitutional Convention. I'm a delegate for the slave states, but I owed your mother a favor."

"How do you know her? How do I know you're even telling the truth?"

"You'll know when you see her. Marta has contacts all over the state. She heard that St. Johns slavers captured a gang led by one Eduardo Dios. I take it she's been following your illustrious career secondhand."

Eduardo rose on shaky legs. "Well, whoever-you-are, I'm not going anywhere."

"The name's Kurt Benedict." The man rose calmly to his feet. He was tall and solidly built, but Eduardo had a few dirty tricks to drop him to his knees.

Eduardo said, "What if the slavers' dogs come after us?"

Before Kurt could answer, Eduardo sent a toe swinging towards his crotch. Kurt turned bare centimeters to catch it on a thigh. Even through the suit that strike should have sent him to the ground. Kurt said, "That one's free. The next one will cost you."

Eduardo grabbed a fist-sized rock from the ground. He waded in swinging while Kurt blocked and retreated, taking blows on his forearms. "This isn't necessary, Ed. Your mom's a powerful person in Phoenix. Would you really rather be a slave?"

"You're lying!" Eduardo shouted.

Kurt landed a hammer fist on Eduardo's skull. The rock fell to the dirt with a thud, and Eduardo sank to the ground, feeling for chipped teeth with his tongue. He had never felt such force from a human blow. "What about Securitas?" Eduardo panted.

"They'll have to survive on their own. Slavers don't waste human capital. If your mom wants to get them back for you, she could always make a trade."

Eduardo held both ears to steady his head. "Just how powerful is she?"

"Things are changing, son. The gulag is coming alive, and your mom is at the center pulling strings. You've heard of the Palace Madam?"

"That's her?"

Kurt chuckled. "No, not Marta. Millicent Drood is the Palace Madam. Marta is her assistant, i.e. the ears and brains behind the Pleasure Palace.

Not much gets by her, and Marta controls four hundred guards for the Palace."

Eduardo whistled. "At its biggest, Securitas only reached three hundred."

"So why did you burn Lake Havasu?"

"It was sort of an accident."

When Eduardo didn't elaborate, Kurt started to pack his bag. "We'd better get started before you freeze."

"My suit!" Eduardo wailed. "What will I eat?"

"There's plenty of food around. After I was dropped in Phoenix, I walked east and lived with some Apaches near San Carlos."

"They didn't evacuate the Reservations?"

"Some refused. Gray Cloud taught me how to live off the land."

Eduardo nodded bleakly, put on his thin jacket, and followed Kurt into the desert. It felt like it was going to snow. They walked along the Cottonwood Wash towards Phoenix, staying off roads and climbing gradually to the Mogollon Plateau.

Whenever Kurt ate or drank from his cat, Eduardo looked over in silent opprobrium. Eduardo thought his story of learning from Indians a boast until Kurt whipped a stick towards a patch of cactus. He skipped over and dragged out a chicken-sized bird.

Kurt pulled the neck and held it up for Eduardo. The bird flapped another minute learning how to die. "Dinnertime, Ed, a nice roadrunner.

Pluck the feathers and I'll show you how to cut it up."

"Could you show me how," Eduardo said distastefully.

"I could leave it for the coyotes."

Eduardo took it by a wing and sat on the ground. With feathers sticking to Eduardo's wet fingers, Kurt shook his head. "This is going to take all day."

"I asked you to demonstrate."

Kurt sighed and gave Eduardo a pat on the shoulder. "Watch the master." As he knelt on the ground, feathers flew like snow. "The trick is not to think," he grunted.

When the bird was mostly plucked naked, Kurt cut off the head. He sliced the body throat to tail and pulled apart halves. "It's better to kill with a stick or catch it in a trap. A bullet or arrow can tear the digestive tract and spill bacteria everywhere."

Looking at the bloody mess, Eduardo said, "Isn't bacteria everywhere right now?"

"Oh, no, the body is very clean. Mouth, stomach, intestines, and colon are all outside the body. They're like the donut hole, food drops into the top and falls out the bottom. Our digestive system breaks down food and absorbs nutrients through the stomach and intestine walls, leaving most harmful bacteria outside."

Kurt cut out the digestive system in a long, continuous, swirling tube. He showed Eduardo which organs were most nutritious. They spitted parts on sticks and held them over the fire. "I've been in the desert a lot lately, but I've never really been camping," Eduardo said wistfully as he chewed on charred pieces. "This is delicious! Have some."

"I'll stick with cat paste for now. I'll have some of the next one."

It was a three-day walk to Phoenix, and as they headed into the mountains, it was harder to find food. Eduardo said he could make it another day, but Kurt took them into the small town of Strawberry. With a pre-gulag population of a thousand Arizonans, only a few dozen gulag cons squatted in houses spread around forested hills.

In the center of town, they found the social hub in a dive bar on Fossil Creek Road. Windows had been broken out during the summer to cool the insides. Now a light dusting of snow swirled in. Drifts gathered on the floor around the tables and feet of the patrons. From the size of the piles, Eduardo guessed they had been there for some time.

Kurt said, "Afternoon. My partner and I are passing through. Anyone know where we can trade for food?"

Although they had been watching since the pair entered, the men could look more closely now. An old prospector with red hair said, "What have you got?"

"Gold, pot, smack."

Eduardo looked over as well; Kurt had said nothing to him. Red rubbed a heavy beard. "I got chickens and eggs. Can we make a deal?"

A young Black man stumbled out of the dark corner to peer more closely. "I don't believe you, man. Let's see the goods."

Kurt didn't take his eyes from Red. "Let's move this conversation to your kitchen."

Slurring words, the young man put out an unstable hand to stop Kurt. "Now, you just wait one second. We're not going to let you get Eric alone to slit his throat."

Kurt inverted the drunk's elbow with an upwards karate chop. As the man screamed, patrons knocked over a few chairs as they jumped up. Kurt said calmly, "Are you gonna let your friends stop your high?"

The Black man stopped howling and struggled to his feet. Pointing with his good hand, he said, "I know you, man! Your were a slaver at Globe!" He whirled around to the others. "This guy's a slave hunter!"

Many of Strawberry's citizens had escaped from slave cities, and judging by dark murmurs, some of those were in the bar. When a chair swung for Kurt's back, he turned and blocked, kicking out to dislocate a knee. Despite the poor result, movement was infectious. Patrons jumped in, pulling knives or pipes from their shrouds.

With bare hands, Kurt struck back at arms, legs, torsos, and heads. He methodically dismantled the opposition while Eduardo hid under a table. As Red was one of the attackers left unconscious, Kurt said, "Sorry, Ed. We'll try the next town for dinner."

"No... no problem, Kurt." Eduardo followed him out of the bar wondering where Kurt learned to fight like that. He never hurried and he didn't even seem winded.

Pre-gulag Phoenix was a sprawling metropolis of two million, with a metro area twice that. Before they could get to the city center, Kurt and Eduardo hiked through Scottsdale, and spent the night in an empty schoolroom at Saguaro High School.

Eduardo made a fire in a science lab sink, tossing in pieces of broken furniture. "I really miss my shroud," he said resentfully as Kurt settled against the wall.

"They'll still have it in St. Johns; they wire them together for solar power. Maybe when this is all over you can head over and get it back."

"When all what is over? There's no endpoint."

"Speak for yourself. In three years I get out through an extraction point."

"You have a wife and kids back in the U.S.?"

"I've always been restless. No time to settle down. As for kids here, they did something to the women. Have you seen any pregnancies?"

Eduardo shook his head. "We're some kind of freak experiment, aren't we? Living in a glass fishbowl."

Kurt opaqued his suit, and slid down the wall to lie down. "We found the right room for it, didn't we?" He was snoring in minutes while Eduardo watched the fire crackle.

In the morning they had a three-hour walk. For breakfast, Kurt bartered for ham and eggs from a vendor. The buildings grew taller as they got closer to the city center. There were a few cars filled with Hank's new gasoline, but streets were mostly empty.

"There she is," Kurt pointed to a stately salmon edifice between office buildings. "The Pleasure Palace, eighteen stories of vice and regret. I hope your mom's home. I don't have enough barter to get inside otherwise."

"I thought she sent you."

"Not officially. I don't even know if Marta's boss knows. It would be bad for business to be associated with the Butcher of Lake Havasu."

"Will I be in trouble here?"

"I don't know what your mom's plans are, but I wouldn't go around advertising. The gulag has given all of us a chance to start over. Call yourself 'Tony'. On the other hand, most cons don't really care what happens as long as it happens to someone else."

In shrouds with a black and gold castle design, massive guards crowded around the entrance. Groups of civilians showed I.D. bracelets as they entered or left. Kurt said, "Those are delegations to the Constitutional Convention. It's been going on several weeks, and I got to get back."

"I do appreciate your taking some time out."

"That remains to be seen. Come on, time to beg."

When Kurt didn't immediately hold up a bracelet, guards slid over to block the door like an interlocking puzzle. The shorter one in front said, "I need to see a bracelet or barter before you go any further."

"I'm on an errand for Marta Dios. I got a rancher here with a hundred cows waiting outside of town."

"Name?"

"Kurt Benedict… and friend."

The man zipped his cowl to talk privately on his cat. When his head emerged, he looked suitably impressed. "She's in the penthouse. Follow me."

Bored guards moved aside reluctantly and the trio walked into an ornate lobby. Few buildings in the gulag had been swept in the last year, but the Pleasure Palace's floors, walls, and furniture were immaculate. At the front desk, a sign listed prices in barter for various services. Just to get above the third floor protel would cost Eduardo's last bag of pot.

Eduardo read out loud, "Baths, showers, protel, fight room, gaming floor, chimera zoo… you have chimeras here?!"

The guard rolled his eyes and led them to a stairwell. Despite the obvious wealth on display, the Pleasure Palace didn't have electricity for elevators. On the staircase they passed through checkpoints and had to explain each time why they had no bracelets. Even the guard in black and gold drew suspicion. Anyone could change chromophores.

At the penthouse, Kurt and Eduardo passed through one last checkpoint while their escort was sent back to the lobby. The open suite of rooms was decorated in business formal with a conference table and comfortable office furniture throughout. There was a small kitchen to the side and a balcony beyond French windows.

Eduardo approached a small Mexican woman in a tan skirt with white blouse. She stepped forward to hug him awkwardly while he searched distant memories for a match. When she spoke with a thin sharp voice, childhood joys and fears came flooding back. "Eduardo, welcome to Phoenix."

Brushing tears from her eyes, she nodded to Kurt. "Thank you, thank you, gracias." Eduardo sensed more affection for the cowboy than for her own son.

Kurt tapped a cigarette out of a pack. "I'll leave you two to get reacquainted."

"There's an all-access bracelet for you in the lobby. Do you need any barter?"

"No, ma'am. I'll get any I need from the game rooms."

Marta dismissed him and studied Eduardo head to toe. "You're injured."

"Broken leg, broken shoulder, concussions, nothing worse than anyone else."

"Maybe you've put yourself in harm's way." After Kurt left, Marta continued speaking in English. She never would have done that when he was small. Was she distancing herself from his actions, or was it a rebuke for how much he had changed?

Eduardo said, "The gulag is full of traps. Even the most careful get hurt."

"You're *not* careful! You're the same impulsive brat you've always been!"

Eduardo felt the slap as welcome relief. He was used to this script. "Maybe if I had a better example, *mother*."

"You had a job in Camp Verde! Why couldn't you make it there?"

"How do you know about that?"

"I have contacts. So? What happened?"

"I was building a security division for the GGC. It was called Securitas, but we got sidetracked up north."

"I thought the GGC formed the Rangers."

"They stole that idea from me! I should sue, not to mention the equity they owe me for setting up the drug and gas convoys. Their leader is a snake. Someday I'll cut his head off and take what's mine."

"Leave Hank Wylie alone!"

Eduardo startled. "You know Hank?"

"Not personally, but the Palace buys gas and gasoline from the GGC."

"I could get you all the gasoline you need."

"You would break it just like you break everything else. Stay away from Camp Verde! The Palace needs gasoline; the gulag needs gasoline."

Eduardo had no army to command, but he enjoyed his mother's discomfiture in thinking he did. After the hits, Eduardo sought a word of reassurance. "If I'm so terrible, why did you bring me here?"

While Marta looked at her folded hands, a tear rolled down her cheek. Eduardo reddened. "Lake Havasu? That was a misunderstanding."

"Oh, come on."

"You weren't there. El Jefe was disrespecting me!"

Marta threw up her hands. "So you kill twenty thousand people?"

"Fine! I'll leave! I didn't want to come here in the first place."

Marta's face constricted. "No, please stay. You can join the Palace Guard."

"Mommy's little soldier? No thanks."

"Prove yourself and you can rise in the ranks. At least stay at the Palace for a few days and think about it. It's a very nice place."

When Eduardo looked over at a spread of food on a table, she said, "Are you hungry? Where's your suit? Have some lunch and we'll talk later. I have a few duties to attend to."

Eduardo shrugged unconcern and walked to the buffet. While Marta left the room, he ignored plates and silverware, stuffing himself hand to mouth standing at the table.

When Marta returned two hours later, Eduardo was asleep on a couch. She shook his shoulder. "Eduardo? Sweetie? I got you a room on the thirteenth floor. You can live there."

He was disoriented from sleep and confused by intruding childhood memories. "Okay, mom. I guess I could try the Palace Guard."

"Oh, good. I've arranged for your new supervisor to meet you in your room."

Eduardo was taken aback, but the disturbing news wasn't over. His mom ran a hand over his head. "I've just learned that Hank Wylie is in town."

Eduardo came fully awake. "He's here?"

188

"You stay away, remember? Hank's probably heading to the Constitutional Convention, but I don't know yet."

"Yeah, the convention. Kurt mentioned that."

"So you'll stay away from Hank? Promise me!"

Eduardo held up three fingers in the Boy Scout salute.

Eduardo's room was no penthouse suite, but it was clean, the toilet worked, and cold water ran from the tap. The hallway vibrated with interesting characters and the promise of trouble. For the first time since being separated from both Securitas and his shroud, Eduardo felt hope for the future.

With a knock on the door Eduardo met his new supervisor, a white teenage boy with surfer hair and acne. "You the new employee?"

Eduardo stepped aside and waved him in. "Have a seat."

"Great, thanks. I've been on my feet all day. My name's Matt, and you are…"

"Eduardo."

"Great, may I call you 'Ed'? I'm supposed to find you a job, Ed. I'm thinking kitchen staff."

"And why is that?" Eduardo said darkly.

"Whoa, whoa, that's not set in stone, but you don't exactly have the body type to be a guard. We've got other openings available. If you don't mind a personal question, do you have a relative or friend on staff already?"

"My mother is Drood's assistant."

"Marta? Whoa, I had no idea. I thought you were someone's third cousin or something. I guess you'll be telling me where you want to work."

Eduardo decided he liked his new supervisor. "What do you got?"

"We could use invisible spies for the game rooms. You have a shroud?"

"No."

"Um, you could be a runner. We always have to chase down guests who run out of barter or try to get to a higher floor than their bracelet allows."

"Maybe…"

"We need caretakers for the zoo."

Eduardo sat up straighter. "The chimeras? What kind? Aergels?"

"And loamins, latbacks. We even have a latback that fights cons. It's hilarious."

"Poor latback."

"Poor cons. Galzilla is two and a half meters tall and could punch through a wall."

Eduardo nodded impressed. "I guess I could check out the zoo."

"I'll let them know. You can start tomorrow at eight. It's on the ninth floor."

Eating alone, Eduardo had dinner at a Palace cafeteria on the ground floor. Matt found him and gave him a t-shirt with the black and gold castle design of the guard. "Wear this inside the Palace. It's better than a shroud design. *That* can be faked. Our guests try all the time."

Eduardo put the t-shirt on and spent several hours looking around. He skipped the zoo because he would be working there, but he swam in the pool, and took his first shower of the entire year. He went to the game rooms and lost his small bag of pot in a poker game. He forgot to ask how much being a zookeeper paid.

Eduardo slept deeply that night in a soft bed, and went down for breakfast early. A Tucson delegation to the Constitutional Convention was eating there also. Eduardo listened in on their conversation. As they were heading off for the day, Eduardo asked if he could tag along. It was only two blocks, but Eduardo wasn't sure he could get inside by himself.

The convention center was a sprawling concrete and steel monstrosity with windows broken out along the second story. Shortsighted cons seeking relief during the summer didn't plan for chill winds in their future.

Many delegations to the Constitutional Convention brought guard teams, with their shrouds flashing city colors. Sharing security duties among them, different groups of guards mingled outside the entrance. There were even some of the new Rangers with green handcuffs on brown suits. Eduardo had seen more than enough of those in Topock.

Sticking with the Tucson delegation, Eduardo squeezed through a gauntlet of guards on the delegation's credentials. In the long concourse, delegates mingled, and meeting times for different subcommittees were listed on white chart paper. Eduardo studied the lists finding nothing of interest.

When he spotted Kurt in a plaid shirt, blue jeans, and cowboy boots, Eduardo headed over. "Yippy – ki –ay!"

Kurt tipped his hat. " 'owdy, pardner! If you're from the slave cities, you have to act a certain way. They don't take you seriously otherwise."

"That's some straight up racist bull flip."

"Don't I know it, and I got serious business to conduct. The slave cities sent me here to make sure that the new constitution doesn't outlaw slavery."

Eduardo spared a brief thought for his comrades in Securitas. "So what subcommittee are you on?"

"I drop by different rooms. It's early days and not much has been decided yet. Right now I'm looking for a fellow named Hank Wylie."

Eduardo was incredulous. "I used to work with him!"

"Your mom told me. In addition to making contact, I'm supposed to keep Hank safe."

"From me?"

"That possibility was mentioned. I thought you were supposed to be working in the Palace?"

"First day. I should already be there, but I wanted to check out the convention."

"In a few minutes I'm heading over to the subcommittee on security. Want to join me?"

"What kind of security?"

"I thought that might peak your interest. There's a debate about forming a gulag-wide law enforcement agency. The Rangers might be the first iteration. If it looks like things are moving that way, I might join. How would you like to be a Ranger?"

"It's better here in the gulag without laws."

"There's not much point in a constitution without laws and enforcement."

"And jails, and guards, and locking people away for twenty years."

Kurt shrugged. "I'd better get moving. Enjoy the convention."

When Kurt left, Eduardo wandered around and poked his head into a few rooms. Dull conversations reinforced his bias against the whole idea of a government. He didn't see Hank, so after a few hours, Eduardo went back home. He was late for work.

Eduardo's black and gold castle t-shirt got him into the Palace, and more of the guards were recognizing him on sight. On the ninth floor, he was stopped by zoo workers guarding the hallway by the stairs. "I'm Eduardo Dios. I'm supposed to work here."

One shouted to an open doorway, "Frank! He's here."

A fat Black man without a suit crunched through construction debris on the floor and stepped into the hallway. "You're late."

"Sorry, my mom needed me this morning. You know, Drood's assistant."

Frank grunted skeptically, and said, "Well, come on, I'll show you the setup."

"Marta said to warn you that she might need me again now and then."

"Don't make me no nevermind. I told that pipsqueak Matt we didn't need help."

Deflated, Eduardo followed. He would have preferred a scolding. They walked through an ordinary hotel room door into a vast urban wasteland of bare conduit and crumbled drywall. Natural light from windows cast shadows on shifting nightmare shapes. Dozens of rooms had been torn apart to leave one maze-like zone.

Frank said dully, "This is the zoo."

"Where are the cages? Where are the chimeras?"

"Eh? They're all around." Frank pointed to a pair of pale blue eyes peering out from under a chair. Eduardo nearly fought for the exit. Frank laughed, and pulled her out by a stubby arm. "She's just a loamin! Say 'hi', Pauline."

The meter tall naked female stood up on hooves. "What's your name?"

"E... Ed... Eduardo."

"Did you bring food?"

Eduardo looked to Frank who said, "That's one of our main duties here; we bring meals from the kitchen. Come on, let's go through."

As Eduardo followed into the darkened rooms he checked his feet. "Where do they go to the bathroom?"

Frank stopped and looked at him. "The toilets, Eduardo. We left the bathrooms in as you can see. Chimeras are people. No different than you or I, except for looks." The Black man sighed and kept walking. "I guess that's why we got this zoo. Most people don't meet no chimeras on the street."

Three latback were chilling by a window. A beam of sunlight illuminated a small stack of rocks on the floor between them. Eduardo had never seen a latback but he had heard stories.

From two to two and a half meters tall, latbacks had coppery red skin and yellowish eyes. When one of the trio tried to stack a rock, the tower tumbled over. In deep voices they laughed and slapped at each other.

Frank said, "All right, Marie, knock it off. You got a new master here."

They didn't look so tall crouched on the ground, but Marie unfolded and walked over. With wide hips and narrow waist, she loomed over Eduardo like a tree. She held out a long powerful arm to shake. "What up?"

Eduardo winced at a grip that could have turned his hand to jelly. "I'm Eduardo. Pleased to meet you, Marie."

The latback twisted a bald head to her friends. "Friendly."

The others grunted and looked back to their game, clearing the carpet for another round. Frank said, "Come on, Ed. They get cranky sometimes when they're bored." As they left the latbacks, Frank added, "That's why you got to keep track of the loamins especially. They got acid in their hooves that dissolve concrete. When they get bored, you might find them three floors away scraping through the walls."

The ceiling had been removed in one section of the "zoo". Aergels had room to flap around, land on the walls, and leap off again, chasing each other in the half-light from the windows. Frank said, "These are the big draw for the zoo. Loamins are like pudgy termites, and latbacks are like cattle. Aergels however are otherworldly. I could watch these girls all day."

"Hey, Frank," one of them piped, swooping by to kick him in the chest. "Any chocolate for Diane?"

"Aww, go on," he said gruffly. "You just wait for lunch."

The girls laughed at him in mocking middle school tones. Frank might be fooled, but Eduardo could recognize death behind those brown angel eyes. He said, "Where are the visitors?"

"We let them in after lunch. Cons have to have a green bracelet or better to be here. I'll give you a list. If you see anyone with a lesser color, ask them politely to leave. When that doesn't work, call the latbacks. They don't mind getting rough. To tell you the truth, I think some cons sneak in here just to get pounded by those ladies." Eduardo could see it. There *was* something undeniably erotic about the breastless, hairless, giant naked women.

For lunch, Eduardo went to the kitchen with a dozen other zoo employees. They introduced themselves along the way, and they all trooped back upstairs carrying buckets full of cooked meats, vegetables, fruits, tortillas, and rice. Keepers ate out of the same tubs as chimeras.

A few of the keepers only ate with other humans, but most stalked off into the dark urban jungle to eat with favorite chimeras in communal tribes. It was only during public hours that chimeras were encouraged to put on a "show" of menacing danger.

Space created for the zoo was about the size of a basketball court. It seemed larger in the dark when you couldn't see everywhere at once. As Eduardo walked through with the other keepers, chimeras appeared suddenly around corners or stopped them with hands on their legs. Food was distributed and Eduardo took his to eat with the latbacks by the window.

Soon after lunch, paying cons were admitted to the zoo. In those same shoes only two hours earlier, Eduardo still snickered as they peered fearfully into dark corners. One of Eduardo's lunch companions groaned, "Here we go," and climbed to her feet. Growling deep in her chest, she lumbered off into the maze of torn drywall.

Eduardo lay down by the window to digest until Frank walked by to kick him awake. "Yo! Get out there and check bracelets. You got the list I gave you?"

"Yeah, yeah," Eduardo complained. "Black, gold, blue, green: good to go. Red, yellow, pink, brown: send 'em down."

Eduardo walked around meeting other loamins and latbacks. For the time being, he only watched aergels from a distance, but he could see how their antics could be charming.

After dinner, one of the larger latbacks named Galzilla headed out the door. Eduardo elbowed a coworker. "Where's she going?"

Sally said, "You've never been to fifteen?"

"Um, no."

Sally yelled, "Hey, Frank! Eduardo hasn't seen the fights. Can I take him?"

Frank nodded and turned back to his companions. Sally pulled Eduardo by the arm. "Come on, the matches don't last long."

On the fifteenth floor, a large area had been carved out from a row of rooms. A bar had been constructed along one side with dining tables, a piano, and small dance floor. On the other side was a fighting ring with ropes and rows of seats for the wealthiest cons.

With liquor flowing at the bar, and a dense cloud of pot hanging in the air, Eduardo pushed through a crowd of bodies to see the ring. Two cons with bloody faces slugged it out for a small bag of coins. When Sally pushed through next to him, Eduardo shouted over the noise, "Where's Galzilla?"

"These are the appetizers, but some nights no one steps up. You may have to fight her yourself."

Pretty sure she was joking, Eduardo preempted any attempt at peer pressure. "My mom taught me to never hit a lady."

Sally laughed and slapped him on the back. "I'll teach you! We can fight each other next match."

Eduardo recoiled at the prospect; she was serious. "Sorry, broken leg and shoulder. I'm still healing."

Sally gave him a pitying look and turned back to the fight. As one of the men weakened, more punishing blows slipped through to the cheers of the crowd.

Eduardo watched a few of the matches with diminishing interest until Galzilla finally lurched into the room with a towel around her shoulders. The crowd quieted. Even fighters currently engaged glanced at the chimera while trading halfhearted punches. Knowing their time in the spotlight was over, they agreed to a draw.

The emcee stepped into the ring, bellowing, "Ladieeees and gentlemen! The Pleasure Palace's one and only Galzilla will take on all comers for the grand prize, a full ten-gram vial of fent! That will pay for a lot of pain relief!"

As the crowd chuckled knowingly, the emcee said, "Step right up and become a legend! Anyone? Come on now, pain is fleeting, glory is forever!"

As seconds dragged, the crowd's expectations deflated. The only movement was the nudging push of elbows and the soles of boots digging deeper into the floor. Finally, one tall, thin cowboy stepped closer to the ropes. He tipped his hat and drawled, "Reckon I'll give it a try."

Eduardo craned his neck to see the owner of the familiar voice. The emcee bellowed, "Ladies and gentlemen, Kurt Benedict! Back again, eh Kurt? I guess you found you teeth from last time."

As the crowd laughed, Kurt kept his gaze locked on the latback. He climbed slowly through the ropes. Galzilla seemed pleased to see him. "Hey, Kurt!"

Kurt tipped his hat to her and twirled it into the crowd. When combatants immediately started to circle, the emcee hastened out of the ring. Galzilla out-massed Kurt by fifty kilos and had a better reach by half a meter. There could be no bombs from the outside. Kurt's only chance was to slip inside those massive arms and turn her torso to hamburger.

Having fought humans several months now, the latback was used to a long period of feeling out the ring. She seemed surprised when Kurt launched himself into her body like a cannonball. Galzilla's fists were too far outside. As Kurt hammered away, she rocked back and forth, slamming Kurt's head with her elbows.

Kurt shook off the blows. When his assault seemed ineffective, he twisted to grab Galzilla's arm in a joint popping arm bar. Galzilla howled and cocked a leg, sending Kurt flying across the ring with a massive thigh.

Kurt was on his feet immediately, but there was a stagger in his step as he returned. His new strategy exposed as ineffective, Kurt seemed resigned to playing out a normal fight plan known to be ineffective. Even so, blows traded would have knocked out any normal creature.

The crowd gasped in awe, and winced in sympathy. A few with weaker constitutions shouted, "Stop!" and "Go down!"

Even half dead on his feet, Kurt would not go down. Galzilla could have finished him or killed him if she wished. Finally, she just stepped out of the ring. The purse was his by rights, but Kurt never collected. It was enough for him to have stood in the ring with the toughest fighter he had ever met.

Eduardo drank for a while at the bar and headed down to his room. Since he was drinking on Sally's credit, it seemed only right to take her with him. Making love, Eduardo's intoxicated mind put Galzilla's head on Sally's body. His admiration for the fighter drew Kurt Benedict confusingly into the mix.

Working at the Palace zoo, Eduardo fell into an easy rhythm. He enjoyed his coworkers, slandered his supervisors when their backs were turned, and grew protective of his charges. If a chimera called out for help, Eduardo would be the first one there with a pipe to beat the con bloody.

A week after he arrived at the Palace, his mother called him to the penthouse for lunch. From the pleased look on her face, Eduardo could tell she was getting regular reports. It didn't really matter, but in a contrary mood, he took the rest of the day off.

Eduardo walked the streets of a growing city. He hadn't spent much time outside since arriving in Phoenix, but feet took him back to the convention center. With his Palace t-shirt and familiarity among guards at the door, Eduardo got into the center without trouble. Finding the same querulous, self-important delegates crowding the concourse, Eduardo almost left again. He stayed for a few minutes with the hopes of seeing Kurt Benedict. Instead, it was Hank walking ahead of him.

Eduardo stopped dead in shock. He searched his feelings, but couldn't dredge up the familiar hate for his old partner. Hank's actions had undoubtedly caused him pain, but Eduardo could admit some culpability. As he moved forward again, he felt mostly a wry amusement.

Dropping a hand onto his shoulder, Hank nearly jumped out of his shroud. "Eduardo!"

"Hello, Hank. Fancy meeting you here."

"I… you… your mother said you lived at the Palace."

Eduardo didn't want to admit he was a humble zookeeper. "We provide security for the convention. Yes, I'm still in security."

Hank looked around the hall for threat. "Sorry about Securitas."

"Easy come, easy go. Well, Hank, I'd love to stick around and chat, but Mom made me promise to leave you alone."

Eduardo strolled off into the crowd laughing silently at the sheen of sweat left on Hank's forehead. Eduardo didn't even want to kill him that much.

For three weeks… four weeks?… Eduardo was happy working in the Palace zoo. Chimeras didn't grate on his nerves as humans did. Hallways buzzed with speculation about the coming election. Millicent Drood, the Palace Madam, was running for Warder. Only occasionally did thoughts of Securitas trouble Eduardo's conscience. When Marta sent word for him to meet her in the penthouse, Eduardo assumed it would be a routine lunch.

When he walked through the door, Marta was wearing her shroud. As she stood at a large table with officers of the Palace Guard, Eduardo knew intuitively that he should back out quietly before his mother saw him. "Eduardo, come over here please."

He obeyed like an errant child, shuffling forward to see city maps on the table marked with circles and X's in red. "What's going on? Campaign strategy?"

"Unfortunately, no. Chimera nests have been discovered along the Salt River. Latbacks are attacking cons and pulling them underground."

Eduardo waited for her to continue. Guards listening on cat radios occasionally made changes to the map. On the southern edge of the city, the Salt River was only a few kilometers away!

Marta said, "As you know, I was attacked by mutant chimeras in the desert outside of Tucson. These appear to be of the same variety."

"Mutants?" Eduardo said, still trying to figure out why he had been called.

"Do you think they came north to rescue chimeras from our zoo?"

"Ours never mentioned knowing other chimeras on the outside."

"I didn't think so, but I wanted to ask." Marta held up a finger. "I'm getting a call."

When she tapped on the radio, Hank Wylie's barely controlled voice said, "Marta, there was an attack at the park off Central. I estimate twenty to forty loamins and latbacks pulling cons underground."

"I read you, Hank. There have been at least six attacks widely spaced along the river. It appears to be coordinated."

"What are you doing about it?"

"Mostly directing traffic, the city is in a panic. People are getting out as fast as they can."

"Roger. I'll see you back at the Palace in about an hour."

When he clicked off, Eduardo said, "Hank's coming here?"

"We'll need him. Until he gets here I'll coordinate a Ranger response with Pedro."

"What about me?"

Marta searched Eduardo's face. "This could all turn out to be nothing, or we may be pushed to the brink. Do you think chimeras from the zoo would fight for our side?"

"Fight?"

"Where do their loyalties lie?"

"I really couldn't say. Chimeras aren't political."

"Pity. Still, our zoo workers have more experience than anyone else. Have Frank assemble the staff. We may need you all to go out and deal with the mutants."

Eduardo gulped and headed out of the penthouse. It had been a few weeks since he had even been outside, and he had no shroud to protect him.

Rangers took the lead while Eduardo's team of zookeepers was kept in reserve. Sightings of mutant chimeras were reported around town, but there were none of the massed attacks seen at the river. Marta had a map of chimera bolt-holes, and Pedro and Jim Dejovine were bringing gasoline and black powder from Camp Verde. A concussive bomb should fry or suffocate the chimeras underground.

Over the next week, an estimated ten percent of the population was driven from Phoenix, but cons were used to violence. Most still had their shrouds, and they carried weapons openly as they had on the first days after landing. The few mutant chimeras that got killed were staked up around town as a warning to ward off future attacks.

Rangers entering Phoenix went on patrol, guarding know chimera holes, as well as looking for new breakouts. There was an estimated population of five hundred chimeras using twenty bolt-holes. Compared to almost two-hundred thousand cons, there should be no contest. Rangers were confident as they drove firebombs across the Salt River to test their strategy. Eduardo followed it all with his mother in the Palace penthouse.

Dynamite was packed inside ten kilos of powder and carried down inside a bolt-hole. Over the radio, Eduardo heard a muffled *whumpf*. Rangers, congratulated themselves until a panicked voice shouted, "Latbacks! Run!"

From the sounds of shouts and gunshots, Eduardo tried to reconstruct the action. The confused fighting went on several minutes while Marta tried different channels to find someone still in charge. Pedro finally called, "Marta! I'm underground! The chimeras dug traps."

"What can we do?"

"Dejovine's still outside, but I'm pretty sure Hank is down here too. Can you send help?"

"Hang on, let me contact Dejovine." *Click.* "Jim, it's Marta. Pedro called. He's underground, and maybe Hank too."

"I saw them get sucked under."

"Can you reach them? I'm still getting a signal from their cats."

"There's no way our men are going down into those tunnels."

"Do you think you should drop another bomb?"

"You mean put them out of their misery? It's a thought…"

"Wait, I have an idea. Our chimeras from the zoo wouldn't be afraid of those tunnels."

"Send them. I'll have the Rangers standing guard."

Marta looked to Eduardo. "Gather your team, and choose your best loamins and latbacks. Wild chimeras may not attack if they're with you."

As Eduardo stood up on shaky legs, Marta's radio clicked. She mouthed to Eduardo, "It's Hank." She said to the radio, "Hey, Hank, I've been talking with Pedro. We're sending a rescue team, but the chimeras have been stirred up all over. Jim doesn't want to drop another bomb until we get you out of there."

Hank said, "Oh, thanks. You can track us underground?"

"The signal is weak, but we have you heading southwest. Just hang tight."

When the radio clicked off, Marta nodded Eduardo out of the room. "Hurry, get moving."

His mother hadn't even asked him! To make matters worse, as Eduardo was leaving the penthouse, Pedro's signal went dead.

Eduardo returned to the ninth floor. By the time he got there, zoo workers were already running around pulling packs together. Marta had called down from the penthouse. Didn't she trust him? That was really insulting!

Sally ran by pulling a latback by the arm. Eyes whirling excitement, she said, "Did you hear! We're going on a secret mission!"

Eduardo nodded and headed further back into the zoo. See how excited she would be underground. As the team was leaving, his name was called a few times. With fear and shame roaring in his ears, Eduardo remained quiet, hiding under a couch.

Episode 8 – Breakout

Mutant chimeras along the Salt River took Hank Wylie and a number of Rangers captive. Eduardo's coworkers, along with some of the loamins and latbacks from the Palace, were called away to help make a rescue.

Eduardo would have gone too if his shroud hadn't been taken by slavers in Winslow. Eduardo was left alone to feed the remaining chimeras. It took four trips up and down the stairs from the kitchen to the ninth floor zoo; no one called *him* a hero.

Eduardo wandered the dark, blasted landscape of broken walls and overturned furniture. He spent more time with aergels who had not been taken away. They would have been no help in the tunnel rescue. Most of all he made countless trips to the kitchen. While he was there, Eduardo caught up on the outside news from kitchen staff.

Mutant chimeras were terrorizing the city, and building nests along the river. Supposedly, chimeras were led by a mad scientist from Uritichs. Rangers dropped a few bombs to collapse the tunnels, but chimeras were too far underground to hurt. The rescue team from the chimera zoo failed in their attempt to reach the hostages. Now, Eduardo's mother was paying a ransom in supplies and gasoline just to keep Hank alive.

After the zookeeper's failed attempt to rescue hostages, the team was kept on standby out by the river. A week later they were sent back to the Palace. Hank met them on the stairs as he was heading up with food buckets. "Finally! I've been going crazy feeding these beasts!"

Zookeepers relieved him of most of his burden, but there wasn't one word of thanks for Eduardo's efforts. Sally said, "Frank died in the tunnels. We elected Jeremy to take his place."

As he was the only one who had stayed on the job, perhaps Eduardo should have been chosen. He said nothing on the stairs, but later found Sally lying on a mattress by the window. "What's wrong with everyone?"

Sally stayed on her back. "What do you mean?"

"I've been getting the silent treatment."

"Are you surprised?"

"I suppose you would have liked to come back to a lot of dead aergels? Someone had to care for them."

"Maybe."

"Besides, I don't even have a suit! I would have been a sitting duck."

"We were all sitting ducks. We left Frank bleeding in a tunnel while we retreated. You have no idea how bad it was."

"I've seen an entire city burn! I was there in Lake Havasu!"

Sally shrugged. "Look, Eduardo, no one blames you. We're just a little raw. Give it time."

Eduardo returned to his room on thirteen to think. If zookeepers were looking for an apology, they could go hang. They should apologize to him for leaving him all the work!

In the morning Eduardo skipped breakfast. He stayed in bed to see if coworkers would call or knock on his door. It would be humiliating to check in with the new supervisor, that punk Jeremy. No, Eduardo wouldn't go back. There were plenty of jobs in the Palace. One thing troubled him though, in that entire week alone in the zoo, his mother hadn't called once. Did she know he stayed home? Did she think him a coward?

No one forced him to get a job, and no one kicked him out of the cafeteria. As long as he drifted in his palatial purgatory, Eduardo decided to enjoy it. He stayed away from areas where the zookeepers hung out, and adjusted mealtimes. He overheard conversations in the cafeteria, and when there was a stir outside, Eduardo ran out with the others.

Two and a half meters tall, and made of glass and steel, a mecha defender sat in the lobby. It had a base of tank tread wheels and a kicker foot for rough terrain. Jointed grappling arms stuck out from the torso, with sensors on both torso and head rotating on independent disks. Defenders were HIGS' hands inside the gulag, but this one was controlled by a skinny Black man holding a radio transmitter.

Visitors and Palace employees stood against the walls as defender and human controller headed through the lobby to a back office. Eduardo nudged a neighbor. "What's that about?"

"They're going to try and rescue the hostages. There's another twenty defenders outside on the street."

When the defender was closed inside the office, spectators ran outside to stare at the others. They seemed to wait patiently for their master's return.

When the man and his robot came back outside, Eduardo could barely concentrate for the excitement. He almost went up to the penthouse for news from his mother. There was nothing stopping him from following defenders to the river to watch the rescue attempt, but to be fair, he still didn't have a suit. Eduardo hung around the cafeteria for news instead.

Hours later, Eduardo ran out with the others. It couldn't have been that fast! Guards in the Palace black and gold cleared spectators out of the way. The Black man was back with his defender, and Hank! He was grizzled and dirty from being held underground.

A hostess met them and waved to the staircase, "Marta's expecting you in the penthouse."

The Black man said to the defender, "Wait here. We'll be right back."

The machine argued, "Why can't I go?"

"We're expected now, and it's a long way up."

"I can climb stairs as fast as you can." Like HIGS, the defender's voice came from a data library, but there was emotion as well.

"You'll chip the marble. Please, just do as you're told."

Eduardo wondered why the man didn't force the issue with his transmitter. Maybe he wasn't really in control. The defender said, "It could be an ambush, Ronald. They may not want to pay you for the work."

The man Ronald looked helplessly to Hank. "Six-four has trust issues."

"To be fair, he may have learned that through experience."

Ronald waved an arm to the defender. "Go ahead then, but don't complain to me if you get stuck."

Six-four tilted its chassis at an angle and added the rocker foot's roller to efforts of the rubber treads. The mecha leaned its torso into the climb and made smooth progress up the stairs. As Hank and Ronald climbed behind, Eduardo had a strong urge to follow. Cut off from Securitas, cut off from the zoo, no job, still no contact from his mother, Eduardo's life had come off the tracks somehow.

Eduardo returned to his room. He led a tentative existence outside Palace society, but still inside the building. Over the next hours and days, Hank left with Ronald and the defenders to chase mutant chimeras escaped from Phoenix, Rangers were increasingly coming to the Palace, and the election for Warder was in full swing.

Fifteen candidates from around the gulag reached the ten-thousand signature threshold to run for Warder. These were mostly ambitious mayors and warlords from the biggest cites around Arizona.

There was Bark Fasbender the slave owning mayor of Show Low, the Mecha Master Ronald Dorsey who chased mutant chimeras out of Phoenix, Millicent Drood the Palace Madam, Davey Wall the Singing Cowboy from Tucson, Hank Wylie the Oil King, and nine others with smaller constituencies.

Phoenix had a population of two hundred thousand, Tucson a population of one-hundred thousand, and Show Low a population of ten thousand. It was a complete surprise when the first poll came out; Bark Fasbender, the Show Low mayor was in the lead. Representing slavers, he drew support from almost all of the eastern cities, and there were rumors that slaves were forced to choose Bark.

If a slaver won the office of Warder, the gulag's future would belong to those strong enough to take it. The United States' worst opinions of convicts would be confirmed.

This battle was already being played out in the final week of the convention. The last two pieces to the constitution were abolition, and the establishment of a gulag-wide army. How these two issues were resolved would have a direct influence on the vote for Warder. Slavers flooded the city to shape the final draft of the constitution.

Although Millicent Drood was running against Fasbender, her Pleasure Palace was apolitical. It took slaver barter as well, and visitors from the eastern cities had a lot of wealth to spend. They donated food for the convention, and delegations bought rooms in the Palace.

Eduardo socialized with slavers in the cafeteria, poolroom, gambling room, fight room, and zoo. To Eduardo, they didn't seem worse than any of the other cons, and he found they were more fun to be around. In his unemployed state, Eduardo was always on the hunt for a handout or free drink. The slavers often obliged.

Late one night, Eduardo was in his room finishing a bottle of homemade prison wine when his mother knocked and let herself in. "Eduardo, we need to talk."

"Did you find me another job?" he snarled.

"What... oh, the zoo... No, Eduardo, I've given up on that idea. You can earn your room and board another way."

After he skipped out on the failed rescue attempt, Eduardo assumed that Marta had lost track of him. Although their lunches in the penthouse had long ceased, maybe she still got reports on his movements. Marta said, "Have you heard of a man named Bark Fasbender?"

"Do you think I'm an idiot? I follow the news."

"So you know what a threat he is to the gulag's future."

"I know what a threat he is to your boss."

Marta shook her head. "Don't be stupid. The first Warder of the gulag must not be a slaver."

"Polls have him up," Eduardo said smugly. "Shouldn't the people decide?"

"This is too important. Eduardo, before the election I want you to assassinate Bark Fasbender."

Marta would never be mother of the year, but did she know what danger she was sending him into? Well, she sure didn't mind sending him into tunnels full of mutant chimeras. "Sure, I'll do it."

"It's not so easy as that. Bark attends the convention, and he sometimes comes to the Palace, but he's always heavily guarded."

"I'll find a way."

"This isn't something you can just blow off."

Eduardo reddened. "Someone had to stay behind and take care of the chimeras! Besides, I didn't have a suit!"

"You still don't have a suit."

"This doesn't involve crawling underground with mutants. There's just one thing. Remember Lake Havasu? Remember all those times you looked down on me for being cruel? Well, you're no better than me. You're willing to take a man's life to suit your purpose. You say it's for the good of the gulag. Who are you trying to fool? If Bark goes down, Drood goes up, and you right along with her. Why bother campaigning when you can just pick off the competition?"

"If that makes you happy, Eduardo, so be it. I never claimed to be your moral superior. I tried to raise you the best I could, but I didn't do a very good job. I see a need for cruelty sometimes, but you delight in it. Bark Fasbender is too dangerous to keep alive. If it imperils my mortal soul to order his killing it's a stain I'm willing to bear."

Eduardo held up his hands. "Don't get all worked up, Marta. I said I'd do it, and I'll be happy to help you out. I just don't want you looking down your nose at me afterwards."

"If you accomplish this, there will be no looking down my nose."

Eduardo went to the convention center to check the layout. Killing a heavily guarded Fasbender wouldn't be easy. Eduardo would need an escape route as well as a way past the bodyguards, all without a suit or camo. Candidate's pictures and campaign platforms were available through the cat, but Eduardo lacked this as well. He found Sally and studied hers.

As Eduardo walked along the concourse, he spotted a con in silver suit. It wasn't Fasbender, but Eduardo was almost positive that he was one of the other candidates. The man had no bodyguard, and he peered down the front of his suit at the cat. Foolish, he should stay aware of his surroundings. Eduardo waited two minutes at the door and then followed him into a bathroom.

There was no one else inside and only one stall in use. Eduardo pulled a folding knife from his pocket. He hit the door with his shoulder and looked for the man's throat. The cowl was completely sealed. The man was typing on his cat, not even realizing that he was under attack. Eduardo heard only a muffled, "Occupied."

A shroud opened only at the owner's pull. The man was safe, unless Eduardo could trick him out. What could he say? Nothing came to mind so Eduardo plunged in, ramming the knife up through the crotch access seam that the man had unsealed.

As blood poured out through the hole, the man screamed and fought back, his hands grabbing down through the suit. Severed fingers dropped into the bowl with a splash. Again and again, Eduardo's knife sought the femoral artery until the man finally slumped to the side.

Eduardo staggered backwards, sweating and covered in blood. He took off his Palace t-shirt, rolled and stuffed it into his pocket. The black of Eduardo's pants hid bloodstains, but his torso and face were smeared red.

The door opened. Eduardo had only enough time to wash his eyes clear, and break free into the concourse. He ran for a fire exit and burst outside into the street. Unlike the Palace, the convention center didn't put a guard on every door.

Eduardo assumed that Marta would be pleased. That was one less candidate in the race, but his mother reminded him that killing other candidates would put the Show Low mayor on his guard. Eduardo promised, only Bark Fasbender, but if he got a shot at Hank Wylie, he might throw him in for free as well.

Eduardo haunted the halls and rooms of the convention center. He shadowed the Show Low mayor, but an opportunity for a quiet assassination never came. Bodyguards even followed him into the toilet.

Eduardo would ask Marta for a sniper rifle, but he put that plan on hold when he overheard the delegation's plans to go to the Pleasure Palace. Constitutional amendments were falling their way, and they wanted to celebrate.

Dogs weren't allowed inside the convention center, but slavers had them any time they went outside. They were good for locating assassins in camo as well as hunting runaway slaves.

Eduardo stayed fifty meters back as they walked the two blocks to the Palace. Their dogs would be allowed inside, but hopefully they would stay with the handlers as groups went their separate ways for entertainment.

Eduardo had no plan but luck. Bark's delegation had dinner and then started up the stairs with their dogs to drink and watch the fights. The convention was ending in three days, and the election held soon after. Seeing Sally with the other zookeepers getting food for the chimeras, he drew her aside. "Sally, I need a big favor."

"No. What?"

"You see that tall guy in the middle with the blond hair?"

"What about him?"

"That's Bark Fasbender, a candidate for Warder. His group is heading up to the fights, but I need you to take him to the zoo."

"And how would I do that?"

"Use your imagination."

"What do you want him in the zoo for?"

"I'm going to kill him."

"Forget it."

"I'm on a secret assignment for Drood. If you help me with this, you can name your own reward."

"Well… I can try. If I get him up there, where should we go?"

Eduardo thought quickly; he would need to vanish a body. "The aergels… over in that dark corner. I'll be hiding around there."

"Just watch where you're shooting."

Eduardo pulled out a knife. "Don't worry about that."

While Sally headed to the fights, Eduardo went to the zoo. Former coworkers weren't happy to see him, but Eduardo used his mother's connections to get inside. He also cleared the way for Sally. A trap was set; all he needed was the fly.

Sally returned with Fasbender but they also had guards and dogs as well. Hiding in a dark alcove near the aergel loft, Eduardo heard them laughing drunkenly and stumbling around broken furniture. Voices echoed through torn walls as Sally led them on a tour, and then a shout or barking upon discovering a chimera.

Dogs were released to chase through the zoo on their own. They ferociously barked at loamins, whimpered near latbacks, and jumped around barking at aergels who swooped down to grab at their tails. When Sally took Fasbender's hand near a king-size mattress, the slave owning mayor sent guards back into the zoo.

Sally took off her suit, revealing no weapons underneath but nature. When Fasbender pulled the zipper to his crotch, Eduardo jumped in behind and cracked him on the skull with a pipe. "Eduardo!" Sally hissed. "The guards!"

"I have a plan. Help me get him undressed."

Eduardo dragged the naked mayor to the loft and called down aergels. He pointed to the body. "I brought you a late night snack."

Confused aergels looked back and forth between Fasbender and Eduardo. "You know, meat?" Eduardo was so sure this would work. Slaver dogs could track the body in no time and everything would come crashing in.

In desperation, Eduardo cut long red stripes across the mayor's legs, torso, and arms. He would eat a piece himself if he had to, but aergels crowded in to sniff. Instinct took over; aergels ripped off chunks with their teeth. Dogs joined in on their next race through the zoo.

Eduardo rolled the suit into a ball, and told Sally, "Go out the back way. Stay in my room for a few days in case they look for you."

"Want me to take the suit?"

"I've already picked out a spot." Eduardo dropped the suit through a hole in the floor where loamins dug through. When Fasbender's guards came to check on him, they would find only a red smear on the floor and a few satisfied dogs.

Eduardo didn't run to Marta bragging. She would find out soon enough, and her surprise wouldn't be faked. Fasbender's body was gone for good, and the suit well hidden. Whether the murder was discovered or not, his guards would get the blame. They and their dogs had been in the very same room!

The slave delegation would look for Sally. They would blame Millicent Drood and the Pleasure Palace for Fasbender's disappearance. There was no FBI to call, and Palace guards vastly outnumbered slavers. The most they could do was complain.

In order to maintain deniability, Marta asked Eduardo to kill Fasbender. She could have sent Palace guards with guns blazing, but that could bring retaliation, or war with the eastern cities. A quiet disappearance was only a mystery. Eduardo worked hard to keep it that way. He spent the cold March night in the park alone. In the morning he made his way to the convention center to gauge the reaction.

Fasbender's delegation didn't show up in the morning; word arrived through others staying at the Palace. Slavers weren't sure what happened yet. They were still treating it as a disappearance. Eduardo was pretty sure that the dogs weren't talking. A few slavers showed up at lunch, looked around the big dining hall, and left again.

Bark Fasbender's removal changed more than the election. Slavers eventually returned to the convention, but without Bark they lost an advantage. As final positions were voted, the two issues most important to slavers were weakened. Instead of explicitly allowing slavery, the Constitution remained neutral. Slavery or abolition would be decided by each future administration.

Fasbender's disappearance impacted a second major issue. The government would now be allowed to form a gulag-wide army of Rangers.

Slavers didn't want any one marching in to tell them how to run things, but they did extract one concession. Rangers could act as the gulag army only if they brought gasoline to slave cities and non-slave cities alike.

The week before the election, the number of candidates dropped from fifteen to seven. One disappeared, one was stabbed to death in a convention center bathroom, three were bought off with gas stations, two by drugs, and one by a position managing the Pleasure Palace protel. There was no law against bribery, in the constitution or in practice.

After Fasbender disappeared, three of the other candidates tried to attract support from slave cities by promoting pro-slavery platforms. This only divided the pro-slavery votes by region. Slavers scrambled to unify behind one candidate. On the first round of voting where candidates were cut from seven to three, the Mecha Master, and all three pro-slave panderers were dropped.

The final choice for Warder would be selected from Davey Wall, the Singing Cowboy mayor of Tucson, Hank Wylie, the Oil King from Camp Verde, and Millicent Drood, the Palace Madam from Phoenix. Before the vote, HIGS hosted a final debate through a gulag wide radio channel. Sitting at the bar in the fight room, Eduardo followed along through his neighbors' cats.

Eduardo couldn't even vote without a cat so his interest in the debate was academic. Hank was running on a platform of prosperity through commerce, easy to say for a billionaire. The Singing Cowboy promised free pot, a stoner's variation of Herbert Hoover's "Chicken in every pot". Millicent Drood promised to abolish slavery and restore fertility, a "law and family" platform.

Marta said that Hank was secretly working to elect Drood, but judging by the debate, he seemed to be fighting for every vote. Appealing to slave cities, the Oil King was the only one of the three who would not take a pledge to outlaw slavery.

The Singing Cowboy was a joke, but he was entertaining and he promised a minimalist, libertarian government. Formed necessarily of convicts, Eduardo didn't think a gulag government would ever function well enough to take control, a strongman maybe, but not an elected Warder.

Millicent Drood was a throwback to the United States. She wanted strong laws and a strong Ranger army to enforce them. She wanted scientists and doctors to figure out how to get women pregnant. Maybe in their deepest hearts cons wanted to live in the type of society that oppressed them all their lives, but Eduardo couldn't see it.

The debate lasted two, long, boring hours. The drinking helped. Marta had given Eduardo a generous allowance to keep the assassinations quiet. He should enjoy the largesse now; after the election was over, no one would care. In the morning it was announced that Millicent Drood had won the election: 39% in the first round and 58% on the forced ranking second round.

Kurt Benedict was at the Palace cafeteria shaking hands all around. As he walked by the table, Eduardo said, "What's that all about?"

"You haven't heard? I've been given control of the Rangers. In the next few weeks we're going to start breaking the slave cities."

It was a government in name only. The gulag had no contact with the outside world except through HIGS. There were no services to offer, and the Warder had no power to tax. The newly formed Rangers would theoretically follow directions, but it was a decentralized, voluntary, paramilitary organization. Kurt Benedict had power only if soldiers chose to obey. Why would they, Eduardo wondered.

The new government may not be able to do much, but Millicent Drood could still throw a party. A week after the election her inaugural bash opened palace doors to the rabble. For one night at least, the destitute could eat, drink, gamble, and fornicate on the Warder's dime.

It was not only unwashed locals who showed up to jam Palace hallways. By holding the party a week after the election, cons from all over Arizona had time to make their way to Phoenix. Eduardo retreated to his room with a bottle and pushed a dresser in front of the door.

An insistent pounding finally got Eduardo up. Pipe in hand, he slid the dresser and opened the door a crack. Sally smiled. "In bed already?"

"Come back tomorrow."

"Party pooper. Take me to see Millicent."

"I'm sure she's busy with other people."

"We paved the way to her election! I was promised a reward!"

Eduardo hissed and pulled her inside as passersby turned heads. Eduardo sat her on the bed. "It's a madhouse out there. I'll take you tomorrow."

Sally stuck out her lower lip. "The party's tonight. I saw Davey Wall in the lobby with his band!"

"Fine," Eduardo groaned. "Let me get dressed, and no more talk about 'paving' or 'rewards'." Sally drew a zipper over her mouth and flicked away the key.

Even a "People's Party" has limits. Eduardo and Sally had difficulty getting to the upper floors, much more to the penthouse door, and much, much more to get inside. Eduardo finally called through Sally's cat so Marta could vouch for them. Once inside, security fell away to the quiet clinks of champagne glasses and sophisticated conversation.

A year ago they might have been sitting in adjoining cells, but Sally was star-struck the instant she walked in. Eduardo sat on a couch, leaving Sally's introductions to his mother.

Although elegantly dressed, Millicent Drood was a short, plain woman with dark hair. Davey Wall was setting up for an acoustic set with his band. Kurt Benedict sat in a corner talking through his cat radio, and Hank snuck up behind Eduardo to put a finger gun to his head. "Bang!"

Eduardo startled. "You flipping bastard!"

Hank sat in an overstuffed chair. "Marta told me how you tried to save me from the mutants."

"Not me personally; I had to keep the zoo chimeras alive."

"Well, thanks for the team effort. It's too bad that we humans are no match for mechas or chimeras. That's why we have to get out."

"Huh?"

"Why do you think I pushed for a Ranger army? Why would I want to put in Millicent and a strong central government?"

"So you could sell gasoline?"

"I buy gasoline from HIGS! I practically give it away!"

"I thought... well, why?"

"So that Rangers can break us out of the gulag. They're going to free the slaves and send them down to Yuma. When they have enough cons on the border, they'll make a break for Mexico."

"What about the lasers from spacehab?"

"Not everyone will make it, but the more we send the better chance they'll have."

Eduardo sipped at a beer can. Across the room the beautiful people laughed in a group while Sally hung on their every gesture. She was a stupid pawn... just like him. The beautiful played games while people like Sally and Eduardo were pushed around the board.

Davey's band started to warm up. Eduardo excused himself and walked over to see the new Ranger commander. "Kurt, can I speak to you? I want to join the Rangers."

Kurt cut his radio call short. "You would leave the Palace for a dangerous life on the road?"

"Absolutely."

"We could definitely use your connections with Securitas. Our first city to break is St. Johns. It would be nice to have slaves help us from the inside."

Whether the GGC wanted to supply it or not, slave cities won the constitutional right to shipments of gasoline. It would provide the perfect opportunity for Rangers to launch a sneak attack. The Rangers chose St. Johns because it was located deep within slaver territory. They wouldn't expect an attack and their militia was relatively small.

With two thousand free citizens and four hundred slaves, St. Johns grew pot to ship all over the state for barter. An escaped slave provided intelligence while Kurt and the officers involved put together a plan.

The timing of different elements would be flexible, but the key to the operation was getting a man in with the slaves to coordinate. Eduardo volunteered. "They'll trust me! Securitas can vouch for me."

Sitting across the planning table with a map stretched before them, Kurt gave Eduardo a hard stare. "You deserted them; you left Securitas to the slavers."

"You kidnapped me!"

"Yeah, and you didn't go back."

"That's why it has to be me. I'm going back now."

One of the Ranger sergeants said, "You don't have a suit. We need a man in camo."

"Camouflage won't fool dogs. That's why it should be me; I'm used to sneaking around without a suit. I can slip into the fields at night and hide until morning."

Field officers looked to Kurt to make the decision. "Eduardo has something to prove; I think he should go."

After Rangers agreed, they proceeded to drill the map into Eduardo's head: electric plant where the shrouds were gathered, slave quarters in the Ace Hardware on Cleveland street, storage sheds and processing building near the pot fields, guard quarters, and the Little Colorado River where they hoped to make their escape.

The GGC sent a single tanker with gasoline. St. Johns was a small town, leaving larger slave towns to wonder what kind of pull they had in Phoenix. With two GGC drivers, Ranger snipers on top, and Los Diablos motorcycles riding escort, the truck drove along Highway 260, passing through the slave towns of Linden, Show Low, and Concho.

Eduardo rode alone, tucked underneath the big tank with a bag full of explosives. At each town, slaver guards inspected the truck and passed them through. Even the dogs couldn't find Eduardo's hideaway.

By design, they arrived at their final destination in St. Johns after sunset. It was too dark to unload so they left the truck at the 24 Hour Gas and Go. Slavers took the company to spend the night with them under guard. Eduardo waited an hour listening for patrols before crawling out of his hole.

In the morning, guards walked slaves from the Ace Hardware to the High School to eat breakfast from their cats. Thirty minutes later they were walked to farms scattered along the Little Colorado River.

Eduardo waited in the bushiest row of pot plants he could find, lying in a soft, green, redolent bed. With all the excitement, Eduardo hadn't slept well. An older Black woman woke him up, pushing him with a rake. "You okay, honey?"

Eduardo tried to remember where he was. "Are there any guards around?"

"Just the usual. You on the run?"

"Not exactly, I'm a Ranger from Phoenix. Have you heard of us?"

"We get the news, honey."

"Good. We're going to rescue the lot of you tonight, but we need some help. Do you know a slave named Ricky from Securitas?"

"Yeah, came in a few months ago. He doesn't work this field."

"Which one?"

"It's a ways. I got a better idea. You just sit tight. After lunch I'll bring him back here."

From out of a pocket, the woman pulled a handful of rolls to keep Eduardo occupied. The one perk of being a slave on a pot farm was unlimited pot. Eduardo didn't want the smoke to give him away, but he gave in after a few boring hours lying still. By the time Ricky found him after lunch, Eduardo's head was spinning.

Ricky sat down cautiously beside him. "Hey, Eduardo. What's up?"

"Small world isn't it?"

"Gram said you were a Ranger?"

"And not even an officer. We came to spring Securitas, and all the other St. Johns' slaves."

"So what's the plan?"

"I buried a bag of timed explosives over by the river. We need slaves to set the timers for midnight and spread them around the fields and town."

"How many you got?"

"About sixty. They're small and not powerful, but we don't need every one of them to catch. These are only a diversion. At eleven p.m., Rangers are going to sneak into the high school, and take the shrouds from the laydown yards."

"No one's going to like that, least of all slaves."

"That's the point. We need slaves to fight back. Chasing after your shrouds will be an extra incentive."

Ricky nodded. "Take the ones from the baseball field. Those are the slaves'. Citizen shrouds are on the soccer field."

"Rangers are going to try and get them all, but we'll keep them separated. While slavers chase the Rangers, our fires will start. This will divide their forces."

"They'll call out the slaves to fight the fires."

"That's what we figured. In the bag are two-dozen pistols as well. They won't hurt slavers in shrouds, but they'll give the slaves some confidence. When the fires start, whether slaves are released or not, we need you to break out and run south along the Little Colorado River. Your shrouds will be down about ten kilometers. Rangers on horseback will meet the pursuit."

Catching him off guard, Ricky shot out a hand to shake Eduardo's. "The boys had almost given up hope. I told them you wouldn't let us down! Thanks, Eduardo, thanks!"

Eduardo's old lieutenant had seemed cool at first, but as he marched off to put the plan into action, it was just like old times. Eduardo had nothing more to do. Guards took slaves back to town to eat dinner from their cats. After dark, Eduardo swam across the river, and hiked south to find the Rangers.

Mounted Rangers on both sides of the Little Colorado waved to him as he passed. They were vastly outnumbered, but how many in St. Johns would fight? It must trouble them to oppress people as they were oppressed in the U.S.

Eduardo stopped at the rendezvous point outside of town where the river veered close to Highway 180. If all went well, the slaves' shrouds should be waiting for them on the gasoline truck. Slaves would be tired from the long hike, and St. Johns guards in pursuit might break through the Ranger's mounted picket.

The plan was to suit up slaves as quickly as possible to help in the defense. This would be the tricky part, finding one particular DNA zipper out of hundreds. The whole company could be wiped out while they searched.

Would slavers kill the labor they relied upon out of spite? Eduardo decided they might, but he eagerly awaited the confrontation. He would be fighting just as hard to find his own suit.

A horse soldier clopped down the road to scout the area. They needed a large flat space to lay out suits for the search. A massive jumbled pile with cons flinging suits everywhere would be chaos.

After the Ranger tied reins loosely to a mesquite bush, he and Eduardo decided on a sandy wash. Slaves could try zippers down one long line, and no confusion or duplicated effort. Eduardo didn't think it would be that easy, but there was that kernel of optimism at the beginning of any large project.

Eduardo waited with the horse soldier, listening over his radio to last minute orders. At eleven p.m. all was quiet. Slave quarters were heavily guarded, but laydown yards for the shrouds were empty. With no solar power being collected, there were no workers at monitoring controls.

Rangers loaded suits for a full thirty minutes before barking dogs brought a patrol. A few gunshots heard over the radio marked the patrol's demise. An increased barking and another scattering of gunshots brought the full guard slowly to life.

By midnight, Rangers were in retreat with all of the slave suits. The horizon brightened with a flickering orange as incendiary devices sprayed burning fuel around the pot farms and onto structures in town. As slaves were released to fight fires, the sound of small arms fire picked up immediately.

While some slaves followed orders to head for the river, a majority sought revenge in town, killing any unshrouded citizen they could find. Eduardo voiced concerns about the integrity of their overall plan, but the Ranger assured him that a massacre was anticipated. It might even discourage pursuit.

The gasoline truck arrived at the rendezvous point after midnight. Eduardo, the horse soldier, and truck drivers unloaded the suits and lined them up along the wash. Eduardo tugged at the zipper of each suit he handled to find his DNA match.

The first slaves started trickling in around two a.m. They walked down the line pulling at seams and yelling for joy upon finding theirs. With increasing desperation, Eduardo started over at the beginning. Coming from a quasi-military background, Securitas' disciplined soldiers were among the first to arrive. They greeted Eduardo with hugs and high-fives before joining the search.

At last Eduardo found his! With trembling hands he pulled it on. "HIGS? Are you still alive?"

"Yes, Eduardo, I'm here. Welcome back."

Eduardo tested radio channels finding his old contact lists still active. At least forty-five of his fifty Securitas soldiers sent to St. Johns still lived. After suiting, Securitas soldiers went to help Rangers fight the slavers. Eduardo stayed at the rendezvous point.

At four a.m., Ricky hobbled into the wash supporting Gram. The old woman turned to Eduardo with a smiling face smudged in soot. Eduardo could get used to that look of gratitude.

By first light, the old Securitas team was back together. For the time being, St. Johns' pursuit had given up. They sent calls for help to neighboring towns, but it would be too late. Fifty Rangers and four hundred former slaves headed south along the New Mexico border.

After walking six hours, the Ranger captain gathered them together on the bank of the Lyman Lake Reservoir. "We'll take a break for lunch, and then you have a decision to make. We're still deep inside slaver territory. Rangers will split into three groups to escort you out of the area. Some of the routes will be more dangerous than others, but you can always go camo and split off at any time.

"The safest route would be to continue south to Tucson. This would bypass most of the towns, slave hunters, and dogs. Our largest group of Rangers will head east to Phoenix. We hope that the majority of you will take this route. We'll pass some of the larger slave cities but Phoenix will send reinforcements if anyone tries to stop us. From Phoenix, the Rangers will escort volunteers to Yuma where the new government supports an effort to cross the border into Mexico. You could be sipping Margaritas by the end of the month."

While slaves buzzed with excitement, the Ranger captain said, "On the most dangerous route, a third caravan will head north and then east to Flagstaff where most of you probably came from. This heads directly back into slaver territory, but I know some of you still have friends up there and want to go home."

Eduardo raised a hand. "We'll take them. Securitas can head to Flagstaff and let Rangers guard the other two routes."

The Ranger captain blinked surprise. "All of Securitas? You've discussed it?"

In a surprised clump, Securitas soldiers nodded uneasily. Eduardo had not said anything to them, and they had just got out of slavery. The Ranger captain said, "Alright then, it's settled. After lunch, anyone who wants to head north can talk to Eduardo."

When the meeting broke up, Ricky pulled him to the side. "Why, Eduardo? What's in Flagstaff?"

Eduardo studied the map on his cat. "Not Flagstaff, Ricky. After we get to Winslow we cut south. With Rangers busy breaking slave cities, Camp Verde will be practically undefended. We can finally take back what's ours."

Forty-five Securitas, six Rangers, and sixty-three slaves chose the toughest route out of slave territory. Most had suits, and with most in camo, they appeared to be a small, lost tribe wandering the desert. Eduardo looked upon opportunistic attacks from slave hunters as training.

A motivated army could manage the three hundred kilometer walk to Camp Verde in four days. Eduardo's caravan of former slaves would take thirty. Eduardo encouraged the leisurely pace. When the eventual destination was revealed, he hoped that Rangers and slaves would have bonded with Securitas, and joined them to attack Camp Verde.

While talking with Hank during the inaugural party, Eduardo realized that the real power behind the new government was oil. If Securitas took the refinery, they would own the gulag.

While Securitas was making the long trek through deserts and mountains, the Ranger war on slave territory turned hot. Eduardo followed the war through Rangers in his caravan. As he suspected there was only a small force left behind to defend Camp Verde.

When they reached Winslow, Eduardo gathered the company together in a park. After a light dinner for a company living rough on the road, Eduardo climbed onto a picnic bench.

"Gentlemen! You have business to attend to, so you chose the hardest path out of St. Johns. I commend your ambition. Because of that strength of character, I offer you one more grand adventure, a chance to own it all!"

Securitas was just as curious as the Rangers and former slaves. Eduardo had let only Ricky know of his plans. Keeping the secret sequestered within Securitas would have been laughably impossible. Eduardo let the tension build before speaking again.

"We are given one life in this world to make of it what we can. You must take chances to make it to the top: be bold, forge ahead with no regrets and no restrictions. No one mourns the old man dying in his easy chair in front of a television. They build statues for warriors who die in battle. Kings are buried in ageless tombs with riches stacked around them."

The talk of death stirred uneasy murmurings among the company. Eduardo knew it would. It wasn't a warning to let them back out, but a prod. Young men courted death subconsciously in a way Eduardo never understood. Something in those young brains equated the ultimate risk with glory and reward. Perhaps every successful species pumped out these sacrificial fighters.

Now to reveal that reward; Eduardo raised his hand. "The enterprise I offer you is one bold strike into the heart of the gulag. While Rangers are away fighting slavers, the oil refinery in Camp Verde sits undefended. We can walk right through the back door. All that wealth will flow out of the ground and straight into our pockets."

A former slave looked askance to the Ranger at his side. "What about the Rangers?"

Eduardo said, "Ask them. Most of the Ranger companies are off fighting slavers and guarding gas stations. By the time they get back, we will be in complete control of the refinery."

When the Ranger nodded confirmation, Eduardo said, "Securitas could manage all by itself, but we aren't greedy. In the last month we've made good friends among the St. Johns slaves. You've suffered under the whips of tyrants. It's time to pay back some of that pain. It's time to get your reward! It's time to win it all!"

Masterfully led by Ricky, the slaves began chanting, "Eduardo, Eduardo, Eduardo!"

Eduardo raised his fist high. "So who's with me?!"

If any of the company remained loyal to Hank, Camp Verde would know they were coming. That wasn't ideal, but by the time Hank could recall the Rangers, Securitas would control the refinery. Rangers wouldn't risk blowing it up in a fight.

Eduardo's call for volunteers yielded fifty slaves and every single one of the Rangers. They would be taking a hundred fighters into Camp Verde.

They spent the night in the park in Winslow. In the morning, one of the Rangers was strangled, and the other five gone. They must have assumed that Eduardo would kill anyone who didn't volunteer. Smart.

The Ranger who did want to take Camp Verde died a martyr to the cause. Well, Hank would know that Securitas was coming. With time pressing, they headed down Highway 87 at a jog. They could reach the refinery in two days.

They turned west in the Coconino National Forest, taking Highway 260 to Camp Verde. With the scent of sulfur and roofing tar floating through the trees. Eduardo thought they were a lot closer than the twenty kilometers showing on the map. A heavily loaded tanker truck rolled up the road. As Securitas melted into the forest, Eduardo signaled Ricky. "Take the truck and driver intact."

The task was easily accomplished with running boards to swarm, and the truck's low gear in the mountains. It still took long minutes for the driver to be corralled and the truck turned around.

Where were the snipers and motorcycle escort? Had gasoline became so plentiful they no longer needed to guard it?

Ricky walked the suited GGC driver along the side of the road. With hands tied behind his back and a yellow-green bump under his eye, he nodded to Eduardo. "I told them I don't have anything worth stealing!"

"What about the gasoline?"

"I told them, it's just resid!"

Eduardo looked to Ricky who said, "It's supposedly what's left of oil after gasoline has been boiled out. He was taking out the truck to dump it."

The driver nodded confirmation. "Our refinery isn't complex enough to break more of it down for fuel."

Eduardo said to Ricky, "Dump the resid here. We'll ride the truck into Camp Verde. It may even get us inside the refinery."

When Ricky nodded sideways to the driver, Eduardo said, "Get all the intel you can. Spare him if he cooperates."

As they walked away, Eduardo said, "Wait, does Hank still keep aergels around camp?"

Confused, the driver nodded. Ricky said, "Why do you care?"

"There are aergels in the hills we'll be driving through. If we can grab a few, we might be able to mess with Hank."

Ricky swallowed indecision. "You're not afraid?"

"I was a flipping zookeeper, Ricky! I've had sex with aergels!"

With soldiers wrapped three deep around the tanker truck, they drove through the final canyons before Camp Verde. Caves high in the cliffs would almost certainly house aergels, but Eduardo decided it wouldn't be worth the effort. Securitas was already there and a massive silver cube shone in the valley like a sun.

Beyond the extraction point a quad-lifter set down near the river on four roaring rockets. At the driver's seat, Ricky gulped. "Things have changed since we were here last."

Eduardo tapped his cat. "HIGS, what is the lifter doing at Camp Verde?"

"Filling up with fuel. We have an arrangement with the GGC refinery."

"What kind of arrangement?"

"That is between me and the GGC."

"Well, HIGS, when I'm running the refinery, maybe you and I will have to make other arrangements."

"I don't understand."

"You will soon. Do you keep defenders inside the extraction point?"

"Yes, Eduardo, it would be useless to attack."

"Useless to attack the extraction point or Camp Verde?"

"I protect my machines. It's up to cons to protect other cons."

"That's all I wanted to hear."

Eduardo switched channels. "Hank, are you there?"

"You're early. Did you get a ride?"

"Since you know all about us, Hank, you know that you're outnumbered. Why don't you just give us the refinery and we'll let you crawl out of there with your lives."

"You may have more bodies, but you aren't getting this refinery. We make fuel for HIGS. That quad-lifter sitting outside our fence could turn you to ash."

"Whatever you say, Hank. See you soon."

When Eduardo cut the call, Ricky said, "We should wait until dark. There's a place near the river where we can cut into the fence. They'll never hear us until we're inside."

"Hank wants to tie us up so his Ranger buddies have time to get back. We go in hard now."

"What about defenders?"

"Drop me at the cube, and dismount the men a few hundred meters from the refinery. As they move in, I'll warn you if HIGS pumps out defenders."

The tanker truck slowed to a stop in a weedy agricultural field where the extraction point sat like a monolith. Eduardo climbed out. He stepped over abandoned rows of beets to put a mailed hand on the ten-story wall of metal. Shroud and cube vibrated in greeting, but Eduardo still had nineteen years left on his sentence. When he gave a thumbs-up, Ricky drove away with an army glued to the outside of the tanker.

Eduardo didn't want to draw HIGS' attention any more than he had to. He just sat at the base with his back against the extraction point. The wall behind his shoulders hummed as if recognizing a part of itself.

Would that day ever come when Eduardo got out? He tried not to think about it. The chances for breaking out of Arizona seemed more realistic than surviving nineteen years inside the gulag.

The truck disappeared down a dusty road, and finally the dust floated away. It took forever for Ricky to call. "We're in position, and the quad-lifter took off. Any sign from the cube?"

"Not a peep. Leave the radio on, and give 'em hell."

Through the radio channel, Eduardo followed Ricky's story. It was better than television. Along with the sound he could feel vibrations in the air and watch smoke or flashes of light. Over the horizon he could just make out the top of one of the refinery's twenty-meter towers leaking steam.

Ricky gave the orders and Securitas advanced. A popping of gunfire immediately filled the air. Eduardo could feel no change in the cube behind him; Hank's threat had been a lie.

Ricky radioed, "Eduardo, Ortiz is at the fence! Any defenders?"

"None. Send everyone, I'm coming over."

The atmosphere changed while Hank jogged. Screams filled the radio. Eduardo slowed to a walk, yelling, "Ricky, what's going on? Ricky!"

Like a rising curtain, a wall of smoke stretched across the sky. Ricky finally answered, "Fire trenches! We're falling back."

"I'm almost there. Don't let the men panic."

Securitas crouched in fields pointing their guns. On three sides of the refinery, trenches burned an oily fire. The river side was still clear, but there was the same wide trench covered by a dusting of sand.

Eduardo gathered with Ricky and the other lieutenants. "Why didn't they light up the river trench?"

"Maybe they tried. Should we send everyone to that side? The GGC would be trapped inside by their own fires."

"Do it, but leave a small crew along the other sides so they don't escape."

Before Ricky could give the orders, a flaming ball the size of a bathtub flew high over the refinery fence. Exploding in a field, the missile started small grass fires. Securitas shouts were filled with fear, and some of the slaves had enough. As they headed out, Eduardo shouted, "Ricky, get everyone to the river now!"

Securitas fought to maintain order while flaming balls catapulted over the fences. Running by one of the balls on the ground, Eduardo kicked apart a pile of burning, tarry rags. *Flipping Hank!*

As Securitas lined up at the river's edge, flaming balls were aimed in their direction. Some fell into the river to be extinguished in a boiling steam. Some hit the banks and still burned. Some hit the oil-filled trench that still miraculously had not caught fire.

As it got dark, Eduardo didn't know what would happen to the battle. The refinery would eventually run out of the balls of resid they were hurling. The trenches would burn out. "We'll wait, Ricky. Tell the men to hunker down."

Eduardo followed his own advice, startling hours later to screams. A random potshot hit a sleeping soldier. While colleagues shouted directions to the river, the burning man ran blindly towards the refinery. He fell into the trench and managed to scramble out of his suit.

The soldier staggered out of the trench, dripping tar from naked feet. A few oily spots on the surface of the trench burned a feeble blue before dying out. The suit was fireproof! Eduardo realized it the same time as all the others. Ricky said, "Continue the assault?"

It was almost dawn. Three of the trenches still burned, seemingly sitting on inexhaustible pools of resid. Ricky's radio crackled. "There's movement inside the refinery! I think they're going to make a run for it!"

The GGC would have cars. Securitas had to shoot them down before they got started. When Eduardo craned his neck, he could hear motors. His cat radio clicked. "Ed, it's Hank. The refinery is yours. Good luck running it."

Overhearing, Ricky said, "We got it! I'll send in the men!"

Eduardo put a hand on his arm. "We need them. Send everyone to the far side. Shoot their tires out, but don't kill the GGC workers."

Ricky nodded respect for Eduardo's leadership. He sent frantic orders as he jogged the riverbank. The GGC was leaving from the empty north end of the refinery where Securitas had few men.

Eduardo rounded the corner when a convoy of GGC trucks broke through a spot in the fencing. Securitas fell behind until the convoy screeched to a halt. Two long ramps were dragged out of a truck and maneuvered into position over the burning trench.

"Go! Go!" Ricky screamed into his radio.

Securitas ran at the convoy firing guns as one by one, trucks rumbled over the ramps. They disappeared through the flames. Securitas soldiers on foot hit the ramps and ran through.

When Eduardo got to the other side of the trench, the GGC convoy was still in sight. He expected them to be halfway to the city, but trucks had inexplicably turned back towards the river.

"Cut them off!" Ricky screamed, taking Securitas cross-country over empty fields.

Like a blind man feeling his way through an unfamiliar living room, the convoy suddenly turned east again. Securitas would catch them for sure!

Eduardo was far behind, his feet slapping in wet sands. It made the chase all the more tiring. He stopped and drew a finger along the ground. In the early dawn light a tacky brown tar stretched between the fingers of his gauntlet. The GGC had dumped resid into the fields around the refinery.

"Ricky!" he shouted into the radio.

Separate fires jumped towards them like lines of falling dominos. It was a trap. But then shrouds were fireproof. As fiery walls grew out of the ground, Securitas soldiers sought escape.

Shrouds were fire resistant, but as Securitas found out in Lake Havasu, if the material got hot enough it would melt.

The men scampered, shucking white-hot suits only to be consumed by fire. A tornado spun above the ground. Walls of fire raced towards Eduardo, turned, and swooped him into the trap. The whole world was on fire. Eduardo's skin stung with a thousand burning scales. He knew the futility, but Eduardo ripped at his seams, exposing bare flesh to the flames.

Eduardo kicked free of the shroud. He hotfooted it over the sand and dove through a glowing wall to find a wet grassy patch on the other side.

Eduardo had found the edge of the trap. Just meters away, the red tornado whirled Securitas' raging souls into the sky. His whole body aching, Eduardo buried his face in the grass and sobbed.

Camp Verde was located in a valley ringed by the Woodchute and Red Rock Mountains. Hank Wylie's oil fire trap was contained to empty fields near the refinery, but hot winds swirled to the hills, lifting curious aergels out of their caves.

The GGC men would come back soon. He had to get away. When Eduardo lifted his head, he thought that the fluttering white wings swirling through the air were aergels come to save him. He dropped his head, moaning softly until first one and then another and another thumped to the ground.

Eduardo could barely move for the pain, but he could raise his head. He could open gummy eyes. Aergels looked back curiously and moved closer, unsure quite what to make of their find. Eduardo's throat was so raw he could barely croak. "Friends…"

Aergels leaned down to hear. Eduardo tried to smile. When he licked cracked lips, he tasted blood. Like a bee sting, Eduardo felt a sharp pain on his foot. He looked down to an aergel with a mouth full of charred flesh. The pain reported to Eduardo's brain at the same time as his epiphany. The aergels tucked in to feed, and Eduardo's weak screams couldn't even reach his ears.

Note to Reader

If you enjoyed the story, I hope you leave a review on Amazon.com. Even a few words would be greatly appreciated. These reviews are the lifeblood advertising for a self-publisher. Thanks!

If you *really* enjoyed the story, a piece of it can be yours! Send a request to dmaswhite4@gmail.com, and I will mail you some of the original notebook writing (until the notebooks are gone).

Thanks again, and happy reading!

Xavier Therg

www.ingramcontent.com/pod-product-compliance
Lightning Source LLC
Chambersburg PA
CBHW071854220626
47052CB00002B/108